Collecting Death

Written by Ron Ripley
Edited by Emma Salam

ISBN-13: 978-1976562655
ISBN-10: 1976562651

Thank You and Bonus Novel!

I'd like to take a moment to thank you for your ongoing support. You make this all possible! To really show you my appreciation for downloading this book, I've included a bonus scene at the end of this book. I'd also love to send you the full length novel: Sherman's Library Trilogy in 3 formats (MOBI, EPUB and PDF) absolutely free!

Download Sherman's Library Trilogy in 3 formats, get FREE short stories, and receive future discounts by visiting www.ScareStreet.com/RonRipley

Keeping it spooky,
Ron Ripley

Collecting Death

Chapter 1: Going Home

Stefan pulled into the driveway and switched off the ignition. He picked up his laptop and phone before he exited the car, stepping out into the cool autumn air. His nose wrinkled at the smell of Fall while he squinted his eyes against the late afternoon sunlight. Hatred burned within him as he sat in the car. Memories he had long suppressed flooded back unbidden. His skin stung from recalled beatings; bones ached from the same. Old injuries, long since healed, flared up again. His stomach growled as he recalled the many nights he had gone to sleep hungry, and the mornings he had woken up still famished.

All of it in the name of his parents' obsession with the dead. Years of abuse and neglect, a cultivation of hatred that had mingled and become dependent upon the devotion and love he had felt for his mother and father.

Finally, knowing he had no choice, Stefan fixed his attention on the house where he had grown up.

It looked no better or worse than the last time he had seen it, which was two years earlier. The clapboard sides were gray and in dire need of a good scraping before a fresh coat of paint could be applied. The windows had a thick film of dust and dirt upon them, old and tattered curtains hung behind the glass, hiding his mother's hoard. Dull gray shutters, which had once been black, hung haphazardly around the windows. The crossbeams of the porch sagged, and the asphalt roof shingles curled up on the corners.

Each step leading up to the wide planked porch appeared as though it might collapse at any moment. Grass had gone to seed a decade earlier, hiding the rotten wooden support posts. Bits of trash littered the narrow front yard. A tattered red and white Target bag fluttered from where it was tangled in the branches of an over grown Rose of Sharon.

Stefan took one final look, shrugged, and then followed the faint outline of the walkway to the front steps. He climbed them casually, unconcerned with the possibility of falling through. Those in the house, he knew, wouldn't let him come to harm.

Others, but not him.

Not Nicole's son.

When he reached the front door, he kicked aside the mildewed pile of mail that spread from the threshold toward the steps. The metal of the doorknob was cold against his flesh, and as he grabbed hold of it, he heard the deadbolt click. With a twist and a push, he let himself into the house.

The air stank of filth, violence, and death. Each smell clawed at his nose, tried to push its way into him and command his attention.

Stefan closed his eyes and listened.

In the kitchen, he heard dishes rattle. Something was knocked over in the basement, the bang reverberating through the lower level. Laughter echoed out of the floor vents, and unknown creatures sprinted in the upper hall. A heavy weight pressed in around him, pushed down on him, and tried to bow his shoulders and force his chin to his chest.

"Enough," he muttered in disgust, and the entire house became still.

He walked into the dining room, the one section of the house he knew would be at least somewhat free of clutter, and went to his mother's chair.

According to the report filed by the police, it was in her chair that Nicole Korzh had been found. Dead of a heart attack at the age of seventy-nine.

Stefan sat down, took out his laptop, and set it up. He turned on the mobile hotspot from his phone and connected to the online world. His eyes darted around the table and noticed a small, windup German toy bear.

Stefan smiled, logged onto Etsy, and created a user account and profile. When he finished, he snapped a picture of the bear and loaded it onto his computer. Within several minutes, he was preparing the bear for sale.

Haunted German Windup Bear, Stefan typed in. *Extremely Active!*

And the bear glared at Stefan, angry at the prospect of being sold.

Chapter 2: At Logan Airport

Victor stood at the carriage carousel, sleep pulling at his eyes. He watched the conveyer move in its sluggish pattern, trying to spot his black, battered suitcase. It came around a moment later, squeezed between a pair of cherry red hard-cases. Victor waited until a young woman moved forward and snatched up the cases, using her shoulder to keep her phone pressed to her ear. Once she had passed him, complaining about the way her non-chip fingernails had chipped, he slipped forward, took hold of his suitcase and got away as quickly as he could.

Even at one in the morning, Logan Airport in Boston, Massachusetts was busy. People met friends and family while others ran for connecting flights.

Victor was happy to be back in New England, looking forward to catching the subway to South Station, and from there to home.

The idea of home, located in Pepperell, Massachusetts, brought a smile to his face.

He pulled his phone from his pocket and checked it again.

Erin still hadn't responded to his texts, which wasn't like her. His wife seemed to live with the phone attached to her hand, especially when he had to travel.

A sense of worry rose up in the back of his mind, and he tried to push it away. She was far from a shrinking violet when it came to life in general, and he personally had taught her how to use a pistol. Her skills with a firearm, plus their home security system and the dog created an almost iron-clad fortress in and around the house.

But it still bothered him that she hadn't texted him back.

Victor stopped at a Dunkin' Donuts in the airport, purchased a coffee with cream and sugar, and stepped off to one side. He caught a glance of his own reflection and groaned. The trip down to Texas had been of the whirlwind variety. There was little sleep and too much debate with his fellow historians. All of it showed on his thin face. He had a two-day growth of stubble that highlighted his pinched cheeks and eyes sunk deep into their sockets from an inability to rest on airplanes. His short hair was a mess and he looked more like he had woken up in a gutter than someone who had just spoken at a symposium.

Victor looked away, shook his head, and scrolled through the messages, searching for the last one she had sent him.

It had come Friday morning before he spoke to some of the other attendees about veterans and self-medication.

Her message had been filled with emoticons and exclamation points.

IT'S HERE!!!

The message had been about a toy. A haunted stuffed animal she was buying off Etsy. He shook his head at the thought, wondering how much she had spent on the damned ghost-infected toy. The idea of having a haunted item in the house was unsettling, and he had talked with her about it before. Erin had been adamant that she would research how to care for it and keep the ghost happy.

But then his worry returned as he realized he hadn't heard from her since.

He had known she had a rotation in the emergency room at Lowell General Hospital, and he had assumed she had been busy.

Now he wondered if he had been wrong.

What if someone had delivered the toy, instead of shipped it to her?

There were stories in the news all the time about someone agreeing to have a stranger come to their house to finalize some online purchase. Victor didn't think Erin would be stupid enough to do so, but if she were tired, she might.

He shook his head, opened the lid of the coffee, and sent her a quick text.

Hey, Sweetheart, I'm in Logan. Should be home in about two hours.

She responded almost immediately.

Who is this?

Victor frowned, texting back, *What do you mean by that? It's me. Who else would it be?*

The phone rang a heartbeat later, a number Victor didn't recognize. He hesitated, but answered.

"Hello?" he asked.

"Victor Daniels?" a man asked.

"Yeah?"

"This is Detective Conrad Patrician," the man said, "are you still at Logan Airport?"

"Um, yeah," Victor said, looking around, the world pressing down on him suddenly.

"Are you with anyone?"

Victor shook his head, then said, "No. I'm alone. I just got back from San Antonio."

"I want you to do me a favor," the detective said, "tell me where you are, and then sit down, okay?"

"What's going on?" Victor asked, panic welling up within him. "Did something happen to Erin? Is she okay?"

"Where are you right now in the airport?" the detective asked. "Tell me, Victor."

"By Dunkins," Victor answered, not sure what else to do.

"Sit down and wait there," Patrician ordered.

"Wait for what?" Victor asked, looking around him, the world spinning. "What in God's name am I waiting for?"

"The police," the detective said, sympathy thick in his voice.

"Why?" Victor demanded, his voice getting higher.

Before Patrician could answer, Victor saw a pair of officers hurrying towards him. They were young men, their faces mimicking the sympathy he had heard in the detective's voice.

"Mr. Daniels?" one of the officers asked, taking him by the elbow. His partner deftly removed the coffee from the other hand.

"Yes," Victor answered, nodding, confused, "I'm Victor Daniels."

The man who had taken the coffee did the same to the phone.

"Mr. Daniels," the officer who had hold of his elbow, said, "I need you to come with us. We have a safe place for you."

"What's going on?" Victor whispered, his stomach churning.

"Please," he begged, "please tell me my wife's okay."

The officers looked away, and one of them said, "I'm sorry, Mr. Daniels. I can't."

Victor collapsed to his knees, his grief a deep, guttural howl that filled the air until paramedics came and sedated him. Before darkness claimed him, Victor lay on his back, staring up at the ceiling, praying for the nightmare to end, knowing that it wouldn't.

Chapter 3: A Trip to the Post Office

They had awoken him a little before dawn and Stefan was not in a forgiving mood. He stormed out of the bedroom, shrugging into his robe as he came to a stop in the hallway. Toys and dolls, books and tools, cooking utensils and bits of clothing filled the bookcases that lined the hall.

As Stefan glared at the items, the entire house grew still.

"I want to sleep," he snarled, glaring at each side, "and if you don't let me sleep, you are going to regret it. You think Nicole was difficult? She *liked* you. I don't. I'll ship you off to a damned monastery. Hell, I'll seal you in a god-damned lead box and drop you over Niagara Falls. See what the hell happens then, huh?"

None of them replied to him.

He muttered a few curses and stalked back to his bedroom. Stefan flopped down onto his bed, stared at the ceiling for a few minutes, and swore. He knew he wouldn't fall back asleep. Anger flared up as he got out of the bed, slammed drawers around as he looked for clothes he hadn't worn in years, and got dressed.

Whispers and hisses filled the air around him as he stomped his way down the stairs to the first floor. In the kitchen, he poured himself a glass of water, got some bread and cheese, and went to the dining room. He powered up the laptop, turned on his phone and ate his breakfast. His bad mood dissipated as he saw a few more people had requested to purchase some of his items. Leaning over, he looked at the list of known collectors and their online aliases. Stefan had paid good money for the information. He wanted to be certain that his mother's possessed items would cause as much damage as possible to amateurs.

Stefan had taken decades to plan his revenge on his parents and he had no intention of failing because he had neglected to gather the appropriate intelligence. Both she and his father had expected – and near the end of her life had demanded – that Stefan take the necessary steps to ensure the continuity and protection of her collection. His dissemination of her prized possessions would not only wreak havoc on the amateurs of the collecting world, but it would shatter her dreams for the pieces as well.

Stefan settled back into the chair, finished the cheese, and wiped his mouth with an old cloth napkin. He checked on a few other items, and answered several emails. By the time those were taken care of, the sun had finished its ascent over the horizon. Stefan stood up, gathered the items that had been sold, and sealed the boxes. With neat, precise penmanship, he wrote out the addresses on the cardboard and placed fictional return addresses and names in the upper left corners.

He picked up his water and walked to the fireplace. Above the dark wood mantle, where his mother's favorite gold-framed mirror had hung, Stefan had placed a map of the tri-state area. Small, red tipped pins marked the post offices in New York, New Jersey, and Connecticut that could be found within one hundred and twenty miles of his mother's house. Stefan studied the map for a moment, then decided upon the town of Uncasville, Connecticut.

The drive would take thirty minutes, give or take, depending on traffic, which meant Stefan had some time to wait. He finished his water, brought his dishes into the kitchen, and went into the room that had served as his father's office. It was dusty and neglected. Stefan knew his mother hadn't entered the room since his father's death.

And that had been in 1981.

His father, like his mother, had collected haunted items. Yet his father's were far darker, their pasts more sinister than most of his mother's stuff. These items, twenty-three of them, stood in a curio cabinet. Ivory cards, containing the provenance of each piece and written in his father's neat script, stood to the right of each item.

The room needed a thorough cleaning, but Stefan wasn't sure if the items would let him. They, he knew, wouldn't listen to him because he was Ivan Korzh's son. No, Stefan would have to earn that right.

He took several steps forward, reached out to touch his father's desk, and jerked his hand back with a yell of shock and pain.

Something cold and sharp had stabbed him, and when he looked at his hand, he found a small, but painful red mark that looked like a five-pointed star on his palm. He flexed his hand nervously, faced the curio cabinet, and gave a short bow.

He backed out of the room, closed the door, and locked it from the outside. Both the door and the threshold, like the window and the sill, were laced with salt and iron. Protective measures put in place by his father on the off chance that the dead might try and slip into the house.

Stefan took a shuddering breath, cleared his throat, and returned to the dining room. He gathered up the prepared packages and brought them out to his car. A glance at the sky showed a bank of dark gray storm clouds. They raced across the horizon, spreading out and threatening rain, thunder, and lightning.

Stefan closed the car door, shook his head, and went back inside for his umbrella.

He hated to get wet, and so did the others.

Within a few minutes, he was back in the car and driving to Uncasville. Traffic on Interstate 395 was light, and he was there in under thirty minutes. It took him several more minutes to find the post office, but when he did, Stefan was pleased to see that there were no other cars in the parking lot.

The rain began, small drops at first, and Stefan was able to get the umbrella open before the heavier rainfall started. He gathered the packages up in his arm, protecting them from the weather, and went into the post office.

A bored, middle-aged man, his face pale and his gray hair limp and clinging to his skull, stood behind the counter. His clothes were a mess, and his wide face was unshaven. There were bags under the man's eyes, and he looked as if he had rolled out of a bar rather than a bed.

Stefan walked up to the counter and put the packages down. He was neither greeted nor acknowledged by the man, and that was fine with Stefan. The postal worker leaned over the packages, glanced at the destinations and asked in a tired voice, "Anything liquid, perishable, or dangerous?"

"No," Stefan replied, suppressing a smile, "nothing dangerous at all."

Chapter 4: Home Again

"Mr. Daniels?"

Victor blinked and looked around.

A young doctor stood in the doorway. It took Victor a minute to place a name to the face.

"Doctor Zhang," Victor said, putting his magazine down.

The man smiled as he walked into the room, sitting down in a chair next to Victor's bed. Zhang nodded towards the magazine and asked, "Anything interesting?"

Victor shrugged, listless. "I don't know. I wasn't paying attention to it."

"Well, you had it upside down," Zhang said gently, "so I was hoping you might say that."

Victor nodded.

"Do you have anyone who is going to meet you here, Victor?" the doctor asked.

"No," Victor sighed, shaking his head. "I'll call a cab. It'll take me back to the house."

Zhang frowned. "I know we've discussed this, and I have to say I would feel much better if you had someone who could go with you. You've been here for a week, and while I can't find any reason to keep you hospitalized any longer, I would be remiss if I didn't say I was worried about you."

"My wife killed herself, doctor," Victor said, choking on the words. "It doesn't mean I'm going to do the same."

"I didn't think you would," Zhang responded. "If I did, you wouldn't be leaving the hospital. What I'm worried about is you being careless, or doing something foolish to your home."

"I don't have a home," Victor answered. He felt rage well up, and he stuffed it back down. "Erin and I had a home. I have a house that I own. A building that my wife killed herself in. It stopped being a home as soon as that happened."

Zhang nodded. He drew a business card from his shirt pocket and handed it to Victor who accepted it with a small nod.

"My advice to you, Victor," Zhang said, "is to find a therapist, and as quickly as possible. Until you do, feel free to call me. That's my direct line here at the hospital. If you can't reach me that way, call the hospital, have them page me and give them your name. I'll call you back immediately."

"Thank you," Victor said. He put the card in his pocket.

Zhang nodded, stood up and hesitated, and then said, "You'll call if you need my help?"

"Yes," Victor said, "I'll call."

"Until then," Zhang said. The young doctor turned and exited the room, leaving the door open behind him.

Victor took a deep breath and forced his legs over the side of the bed. Each movement was a challenge, sorrow and grief pulling at him, threatening to drag him down to the floor. He fought the urge, gathered up his few belongings, and made his way out of the room. His steps were ponderous, the world a dull blur around him. He followed the signs to the elevators, took one down to the main floor, and used the phone at the security desk to call for a cab.

Soon, without remembering how it had occurred, Victor found himself in the back of a cab. The driver was silent, a news station playing softly on the radio. Victor turned his attention to the world beyond the car's dirty glass. He recognized some of the streets and realized they were already in Pepperell, and he wondered how long he had been sitting in silence.

A shuddering breath raced from his lips, the cabbie turning onto Pine Street. Within a matter of seconds, the man had stopped the car in front of number 71, Victor's house.

"What's the fare?" Victor managed to ask.

The cabbie, an old man with hair a sickly yellow, shook his head. "You're good, kid. One of the doctors called up my dispatcher and took care of it."

Victor blinked, confused, and then said, "Oh."

He sat for a moment longer, then dug out his wallet and pulled a twenty. In silence, he passed the bill to the cabbie. The man hesitated for a heartbeat before he nodded and accepted it. No more words were exchanged between them as Victor exited the cab and stood on the sidewalk in front of the house. He remained there, suitcase in hand as the cabbie pulled away.

Victor's heart raced, and he shuddered. He ground his teeth together, clenched his jaw, and followed the cobblestone walkway to the front steps. His legs trembled as he climbed the cement stairs and his hands shook as he got out his house key. Three times it took him to fit the key into the deadbolt and let himself in.

He stood completely still in the doorway, imagining that he could smell the gas from the oven.

Victor remembered his first conversation with Doctor Zhang and the man's reluctance to speak about how Erin had killed herself.

Herself and the two cats.

Like Sylvia Plath, Zhang had told him. Erin had blown out the pilot light and turned on the gas in the oven. Then she had put her head in it, inhaling the deadly fumes until she died. The gas had spread through the house, killing the cats in the upper bedroom where they slept on the bed.

The neighbors had smelled gas and called the utility company and fire department. Erin had been dead for almost a day before the gas had been turned off and the fire fighters had found her body.

Her body, Victor thought, shuddering at the image.

She was still in the morgue, at Zis Sweeney Funeral Home in Nashua, New Hampshire where her family was from. Her parents had contacted the Home, and they were waiting for Victor to be recovered enough to attend the wake and funeral.

The most terrifying aspect of Erin's death was the lack of a reason. She hadn't left a note. Nor had she ever even expressed a morbid interest in suicide. It had never been a subject of conversation between them. She had been happy in her job, working as a librarian, collecting her books and items people told her were haunted.

Victor shuffled the rest of the way into the house and shut the door behind him. He didn't bother to lock it as he let the suitcase fall to the floor. As though of their own accord, his feet carried him into the kitchen. Dirty dishes were on the counter. The trash stank. Above the sink, the leaves of the spider plant drooped for need of water. The door to the oven was open, his chair dragged close to it.

An image of her sitting on his chair, her body bent in half, and her head stuffed deep into the confines of the oven.

Victor staggered forward, jerked the chair out, and sat down, the wood shaking beneath him. He closed his eyes and pressed his hands against them. Each breath was painful as if a heavy weight had been dropped onto his chest. He dragged air in through his nose and between his teeth, fighting back despair.

Finally, after several minutes, he regained his composure and straightened up.

He opened his eyes, and they locked onto something strange.

An old toy bear sat upright in the center of the table. The fur was thin in some spots, the arms and legs stiff. It looked old, the sun glowing in its dull glass eyes.

Victor straightened up.

It wasn't the sun he saw in the toy's eyes.

It couldn't be.

The shades were drawn in the kitchen. What little light there was came in through the door that led to the game room, and that was behind the bear.

Victor sat back, and as he did so, the toy's eyes followed him.

Chapter 5: A Home for Anne

Grant Ross had a penchant for dolls.

Not all dolls.

Grant had a very specific taste. He collected rare, French bisque dolls, and he had adapted his apartment to care for the unique collection. His job as an interior designer afforded him not only the funds, but the time to dedicate to his passion. A passion reflected in his home.

Of the several thousand square feet that his apartment boasted, fully eighty-five percent of it was dedicated to his dolls, or his 'girls', as he preferred to call them.

He had seventy-six of them, divided into three different rooms. Each room was designed to reflect the type of dolls it housed. The dolls were separated and protected within individual glass cases. Temperature and humidity controls ensured that the dolls were kept in a pristine environment.

Grant had even had large battery packs installed to prevent possible damage to the dolls should a blackout occur. He had moved down to New Orleans from Manhattan, all to better care for his dolls, and to understand them as well.

Some of them, he was certain, were haunted. Yet no matter how many mediums or voodoo priests and priestesses he brought in, none of them confirmed his suspicions.

Grant rolled his eyes at the idea of his girls being so mundane as to be barren of ghosts and spirits.

Good God, he thought, sitting down at his laptop with a glass of pinot noir, *you would think that in New Orleans I would learn at least one of the girls was a little more than what she looked like.*

He sighed and typed in his password with one long, manicured finger. After several sips of wine, he settled back into his chair and glanced at his email. He was nearly halfway through his account when he saw an instant message from Etsy.

Haunted Doll for Sale! Bisque!

Grant snorted at the Bisque typo and quickly followed the link to Etsy. Early on he had learned that many people couldn't spell, and that was just as true whether someone was trying to tell him what they wanted their kitchen to look like, or were describing an item for sale. All of his search parameters included common misspellings, and more than one of his girls had been purchased that way.

Grant looked at the item listed for sale.

His hands shook so badly he had to set his wine glass down.

Not only was he looking at a Bisque, but one of the finest he had ever seen. She had blonde hair with tight ringlets, a delicately painted face, and what looked like original clothes and shoes. The seller, NA Sante, listed the price at two thousand dollars.

A more than reasonable request.

Grant hated to wait, so he sent the seller a message stating that he was willing to send the money immediately if the seller was amicable to the idea.

The response came less than thirty seconds later.

Send it along, and Anne is all yours!

Grant transferred the funds as quickly as he could and sent back a message with the confirmation number for the transaction.

Thank you very much! the seller wrote. *She is a beautiful girl, but she is rather precocious. I will pack her bags, and she will be on her way in the morning.*

Grant chuckled, picked up his glass with a hand that had ceased to shake, and wrote, *I'm more interested in her status as a Bisque than I am in any paranormal attributes she might have.*

The seller responded with a smiley face emoticon and the words, *Well, I think you'll enjoy them both. Thank you again for your business!*

Grant thanked the seller in return and finished his wine. A statement the seller had made came back to him.

Her bags, Grant thought excitedly, *does she come with clothes? All of them?*

The smile that spread across his face was one of sheer joy.

Chapter 6: An Interruption

Stefan had finished an argument with Anne and packed her up for the next morning when a knock came at the door.

The constant mumbling, whining, and groaning from the dead bound to the various knick knacks scattered around the house came to a sharp stop.

Stefan stood up and walked to the front door as the person on the other side knocked again. Stepping to the left and stopping several feet from the door, Stefan called out, "Who is it?!"

"Is this Mr. Stefan Korzahn?" a man asked.

"Who are you?!" Stefan demanded.

"Mr. Korzahn," the man said, "if you could just open the door and let me in, I know that we could conduct business in a satisfactory manner."

"Tell me who you are," Stefan snarled, "or I will come out there and drive you off my property with a stick."

A note of fear could be heard in the man's voice as he said, "Mr. Korzahn, my name is Aldo Collier, and I am interested in some of the items your mother collected over the years. She and I often faced each other across the aisle of various auction houses, and I had hoped to be able to come and speak to you about purchasing your mother's collection."

Stefan recognized the name and put a face to it as well. His mother had shown him a photograph years before. Mr. Collier was a short, round man who looked as though he could never find a set of clothes that might fit him. A neck roll of fat had hung over the collar of his shirt, his hair had been thin, and his eyes had held a nasty gleam. The man's thin lips had echoed the man's foulness hinted at by his eyes, and Stefan knew that he would gain nothing by attempting to negotiate a deal with the man.

"They're not for sale," Stefan lied. "Get out."

"Now Mr. Korzahn," the man said hastily, "let's not make such a blanket statement. I'm certain that you would be willing to part with some of your mother's possessions, should there be enough of a financial incentive to do so."

"Mr. Collier," Stefan said through clenched teeth, "I have a Louisville Slugger baseball bat in my hand. By the time I count to five, I am going to unlock my door, come outside, and use you as batting practice. Am I understood, Mr. Collier?"

There was a nervous, frightened tremble in Collier's voice as he replied, "Yes. Yes, I understand. I'll just leave my business card here on the porch. Please give me a call should you have a change of heart regarding your poor, deceased mother's possessions."

Stefan didn't respond. He listened, and not until he heard Collier walk down the decrepit front steps did Stefan walk to the dirty sidelights. With his hand on the doorknob, Stefan peered out after the man.

Collier was dressed in a ridiculous sky blue suit, a matching fedora on his head. The man had a bowlegged walk, which made him look like a duck waddling across the road. As Stefan watched, the man stopped at a bright yellow Lexus Sportster, climbed in and raced off.

The license plate, Stefan saw, was from Vermont and read 'GHO5T5.'

Stepping away from the sidelights, Stefan rubbed the stubble on his chin and wondered if he might need to find out Collier's house and pay the man a visit. Or at least drop off an item. One that would silence Collier forever. Stefan didn't want any of his mother's possessed items tucked safely away in the home of some collector who knew what it was they were purchasing. He wanted the amateurs to buy them. The ones who wouldn't know how to protect themselves against the death they were bringing.

Stefan considered the idea of Collier's murder as he went to the kitchen for something to eat, the noise level of the house increasing steadily.

When he reached the kitchen, he poured himself a glass of water.

He's not worth one of the dead, Stefan decided. *I'll strangle him if he shows up again.*

Chapter 7: Alone with a Bear

When he and Erin had moved into their house, Victor had turned a large portion of the basement into a library. The constant whirr of dehumidifiers was a comforting sound, reminding him that his precious books were protected. In temperature-controlled cases were some of his more expensive pieces of militaria.

Victor had carried Erin's new toy down into his library, set the bear upon a small table, and sat down across from it in his reading chair.

He had sat there for days. Victor brought his meals down and ate in front of it. He used the downstairs bathroom when necessary, and he hadn't showered since he had returned home.

And whenever he looked at the bear, it stared back at him.

Victor knew it would speak to him, it was only a matter of when, and he didn't want to miss it. He knew the toy had been a participant in Erin's death. The knowledge was instinctual, a primal response to the strange sensation he had when near the bear.

Victor drummed his fingers on his knee, fighting sleep. He was exhausted, depressed, and angry. Days before, he had taken the clock out of his library and put it in the kitchen. He had left his watch and phone there as well. The bear, and nothing but the bear, occupied his attention. He ate so he could stay alive to catch the toy in some unnatural act. Anything.

The bear moved.

Victor forced his fingers to keep up their routine, kept his eyes dull and unfocused while out of the corner of them he watched the toy.

With infinite patience, the bear's head turned, centimeter by centimeter until it stared at him. Then its mouth opened, which Victor hadn't thought was possible.

The voice that slipped out was horrifyingly sweet. It was exactly the way a child might imagine a toy to speak.

"You are Victor," it whispered.

He didn't respond.

"Oh yes, you are." A soft giggle followed the statement. "Did you know she called for you, before the end? She was confused. So confused, Victor. Sometimes she thought I was her sister. Did you know she had a sister, Victor? No, I imagine you did not. You are not special. Not the way I am."

Victor's lip twitched, and he knew the bear had seen it, for it ceased to talk. When he looked at the toy straight on, the muzzle was closed again. The head was turned away. Victor almost didn't believe what he had heard. He couldn't believe it.

You're imagining things, he scolded himself. *You would have known if Erin had a sister. She would have told you.*

Victor closed his eyes and pressed the heels of his hands against them until stars burst around the edges of the darkness. He took long, shuddering breaths, trying to calm himself.

Then he dropped his hands and straightened up. He opened his eyes, blinked, and thought, *her papers. If she had a sister, then the information would be in her papers.*

Victor stood up and staggered out of the room. His body ached from the days he had spent in the chair, the muscles in his legs protesting loudly as he climbed upstairs to the second floor. Erin had her own room where she kept her haunted knick-knacks and her important papers. Parts of her life she had never wanted to talk about or share with Victor.

He twisted open the door, shoving it aside and flicking on the light. The bright glow of the desk lamp made him blink, and he hesitated a moment to gather himself. In the far right corner of the room was a small, wooden filing cabinet. Within its two drawers would be any information about a sister, if there had ever been one.

He stomped over the cabinet, reached out and took a brass drawer pull in his hand, and then stopped. Victor realized that one of two results were possible after he opened the drawer. The first was that there was no deceased sister. If that was the case, he would have to return to the hospital and check himself in for an indefinite period of time.

Should he find evidence of a dead sibling, then it meant there was a haunted toy in his library.

Victor swallowed once and tugged the drawer open.

During Erin's life, he had never considered such an invasion of her privacy, and even with her dead, he found it hard to look through the files she had held as private and confidential. The first drawer yielded nothing, and he slammed it closed. With growing fear and anger he ripped open the second, jerking the drawer right off its tracks, so it landed with a thud on the hardwood floor.

His eyes landed on a single, thin manila folder. It had the name 'Emily' written on it in Erin's delicate script. Victor was surprised at how steady his hands were as he extracted the folder and opened it.

Within, he found photographs and two pieces of paper. The pictures were of Erin when she was a little girl, images he had seen before. But instead of her standing alone beneath an elm tree, or leaning against an old Buick sedan, she was with a girl who was a few inches taller. A few years older. There was no denying the family resemblance between Erin and the other girl.

They shared the same cheekbones and narrow nose. Fine, arched eyebrows and dirty blonde hair. A slim build and a single dimple in the right cheek of each as they smiled.

Victor felt numb as he examined the papers.

The first was a birth certificate for one Emily Ann King. She had been born two years to the day before Erin.

The second was a death certificate for one Emily Ann King.

She had died two weeks after her sixteenth birthday. The cause of death was blunt force trauma to the head.

Victor returned the certificates and photographs to the folder, placed the folder on Erin's desk and stood up. Waves of nausea washed over him, forcing him to sit down in her chair. He found himself staring at the dark screen of her laptop, considering the fact that there was a haunted toy in his library.

For a long time, he remained in the chair. Finally, Victor leaned forward, turned on the laptop, and punched in Erin's password. When he had accessed the internet, Victor brought up a search engine and typed in his request.

How to destroy a possessed toy?

Chapter 8: Too Much Information

For the first time in days, Victor sat on his porch. He was in his rocking chair, Erin's empty chair beside him. The streetlights had come on, the new LED bulbs casting cones of pale light down onto the pavement.

In his ears, Victor heard the normal sounds of life. A world unaffected and untroubled by the death of his wife. The loss of Erin, his best friend, meant nothing to anyone.

Children rode their bicycles along the street, others walked by and talked on their cellphones or texted. Mr. Murphy, two houses up, was mowing his lawn. Three doors down to the right, Mr. and Mrs. Sullivan screamed at each other, their raised voices faint against the ambient noise of the neighborhood.

Victor knew that everyone on the street was aware of Erin's death. Not only had they seen the fire engines and other emergency vehicles, but they had also watched the news. Reporters from the local papers and television stations had interviewed them about the event, as well as about Victor and Erin's relationship.

Everyone knew she had killed herself.

And so no one said anything about it.

People who had known Victor and Erin as a couple waved as they went past, but they didn't stop to chat. Their smiles were strained as they picked up the pace, hurrying along to the next lot.

Victor couldn't blame them. But he couldn't forgive them either.

Not a single person had given their condolences.

He closed his eyes and leaned back in the rocker, moving the chair gently, his feet planted on the porch floor. Victor considered what he had read online. The information he had gathered for hours.

And there had been much more for him to delve into.

Too much.

Within half an hour, he was lost in a tangled skein of hearsay, rumor, and documentaries he wasn't quite sure were real. What he had learned, in the end, was that he hadn't learned anything at all. He needed to speak to someone reputable, who had destroyed haunted items before.

Victor opened his eyes, stood up and went back into the house. As the door closed behind him, he felt uncomfortable, as though a weight had settled around his shoulders and tried to drag him to the floor. He frowned and looked around, trying to pinpoint the source of the sensation.

A moment later, he located it.

There was the sound of whispering. A low, sweet voice speaking from the basement. The words were inaudible, and Victor approached the closed door with trepidation. He placed his ear against the wood and listened.

"Victor," the bear said, "why are you still here? She didn't leave because she couldn't. I told her what to do and when to do it. You're not like that. Or are you? Do you want me to tell you what to do, Victor? Why don't you come downstairs? There's a gas line down here. You could open it up. So easy. Then you could sit down by the furnace and wait. It won't take long. Not long at all. Your cats lasted longer than your wife, Victor. Come down and see if you will too. It's alright if you don't. Think about it. The quicker you give in and let yourself die, well, that means you'll be with your beloved all the sooner. Yes?"

Victor gasped at the pain the bear's words caused him. It was as if each idea was a needle, one that plunged deep into his heart and dragged a length of barbed wire with it. The bear's voice was insistent, the ideas poisonous and sweet in the same breath. Part of Victor longed to do as the bear said; to descend the stairs and to end it all to join Erin.

Yet a deep resolve rose up in him from some secret part he had never accessed before. It was a strength that felt true and hereditary. As if it had always been his, but never needed.

Dipping into that resolve, Victor pushed himself away from the door, fell against the arm of the couch, and dropped into it. He stared at the door, horrified not at what he had heard, but at the willingness a part of him felt towards the bear's suggestions.

Victor climbed off the couch and walked with all of the grace and poise of a drunk up to Erin's private room. He logged onto the computer again and searched for paranormal specialists near Pepperell, Massachusetts.

The closest he found was a man by the name of Jeremy Rhinehart in Brookline, New Hampshire. According to the man's website, Mr. Rhinehart specialized in paranormal abatement in regards to possessed, cursed, and haunted items.

Victor considered the bear in the basement and thought the toy could possibly fit into all three categories.

At the bottom of the website, he found a link to contact Mr. Rhinehart. It was a standard email form which required Victor to include basic personal information, and any experience he had with the paranormal.

The first part was easy.

When he came to the personal experience he hesitated, swallowed his pride, and wrote, *a haunted toy convinced my wife to kill herself.*

Victor didn't read through the statement but merely clicked on the send button. After he had finished, he sat back in Erin's chair, looked at his cellphone and wondered if the man would call him back.

He hoped so because the bear's voice was growing louder.

Chapter 9: Interrupted

Stefan sank in his chair and stared at a book.

It was a battered copy of *The Tale of Peter Rabbit*, and it had killed three children Stefan knew of. His mother had kept it locked away in her bedroom, within a safe in the wall. The one she didn't think Stefan had known about.

He had, but only because he had been angry about his college money; the cash his father had squirreled away in various safety deposit boxes over the years. Money meant to give Stefan a good start on life and keep him out of the factories. Stefan had already been in the army for two years by the time his mother had dipped into his college fund, but that didn't matter to Stefan.

He had been forced into the army, a choice given to him by a local judge who told him he could serve two years in prison for possession of marijuana, or he could go into the armed services.

Stefan had chosen the army over prison, although there were times during his enlistment where he doubted the sanity of his decision. Prisoners, he had decided, had more rights than soldiers did.

Or at least that's what it felt like.

Not that it had mattered. Stefan had done two years in the infantry, learned how to carry too much weight and march until he was asleep and still on the move. He had learned skills he had never put into practice, and that were no good in the world outside of the army. And since he had lacked the intellectual ability to be promoted, Stefan had been forced out.

During the time in the army, he had often thought about what he would do with the college money. Part of him wanted to buy a brand new Ford Mustang and drive it from the East Coast to the West Coast, up into Canada, over to Alaska, then all the way down into Mexico.

Those plans had been shot down when he got out of the service and discovered his mother had purchased a bigger home for her haunted knick-knacks. All of it done with his college money.

And what she hadn't spent on the house, she had used for the purchase of more haunted items.

Stefan had been put out by the entire situation and had refused to see his mother for years afterward.

The Tale of Peter Rabbit had been one of the items his mother had purchased with his money.

He wrapped it in tissue paper, placed it within a padded envelope, and sealed it. Part of him hoped that the people who bought it didn't have children.

But a larger part simply didn't care.

Everyone could suffer the way he had. If not financially, then emotionally and spiritually. He smiled and chuckled as he added the shipping label to the envelope's top and set it aside.

His cellphone rang, and Stefan looked down at it, anxiety flooding through him.

The caller ID showed a number he didn't recognize as he answered it cautiously.

"Hello?" he asked.

"Hello, Mr. Korzh!" a man said cheerfully. "This is Aldo Collier, we spoke a few days ago through your mother's front door."

The man chuckled at his own joke, stopping once he understood Stefan wasn't joining in.

Mr. Collier cleared his throat and said, "I was calling to see if you had thought any more about my proposition."

Stefan cut him off, saying, "How did you get this number?"

"Well," the other man said with forced cheerfulness, "a true collector doesn't let something as paltry as an unlisted phone number stop him from obtaining what he wants."

"Don't ever call me again," Stefan said and ended the call.

The phone rang a heartbeat later, and Stefan answered it.

"I'm going to keep getting in touch with you," Mr. Collier said, a note of determination in his voice. "I want some of those pieces, sir, and I will have them."

Stefan pressed 'end' and blocked Collier's number. He shook his head.

He would have to take care of the man after all.

Chapter 10: A Helpful Call

Victor lay in his bed, the phone beside him on the pillow. He had been unable to sleep, despite the exhaustion threatening to overwhelm him. Through the house, he heard the soft, unintelligible mutterings of the bear. Victor knew what the toy wanted him to do, but he wouldn't.

The toy was dangerous, which meant Victor could not, in good conscience, throw it away. He had thought about trying to burn it in the oven, or taking a hammer to it and burying it in the backyard. But neither of those options was a guarantee that the bear would stop. From what he had read, Victor learned there was the possibility he could make the situation worse by freeing it.

No, he had to wait and hope the man got back to him.

There was little chance of the specialist contacting him Victor feared, as he looked at the clock on the bedside table. It was already past two in the morning, and any sane person was already asleep.

His phone rang, cutting through his exhaustion.

Victor snatched it up and answered it without a glance at the caller ID.

"Hello?" he said.

"Hello, this is Jeremy Rhinehart," a man said. "You sent me an email."

"I did," Victor said. "Can you help me?"

"Tell me what's going on," Jeremy said.

Victor did. Everything from the text message Erin had sent him to the bear's mutterings in the deep stillness of the early morning.

There was a note of concern when Jeremy spoke again.

"I'm out of town," the man said, "and I won't be back for several days. I'll call you as soon as I return, but in the meantime, you are going to have to contain the bear. I know this is unlikely, but do you have any lead in the house?"

"No," Victor said, shaking his head, "Why?"

"You need to get some," Jeremy said. "Go to an antique store and look for an old safe. Even a children's toy safe from the thirties or older. If you don't have any luck there, try junkyards in the area. When you find one, put the bear in the safe. But be careful. Wear gloves."

"I've already touched it without gloves," Victor said, fighting back a sense of rising panic. "Was I wrong?"

"No, but you were lucky," Jeremy said. "And leave the house now. Go and get a hotel room for the rest of the night. Sleep if you can, and then find the lead. Do not go back to your home until you do so. Is that understood, Victor?"

"Yes, yes it is," Victor answered.

"Excellent," Jeremy said. "I am sorry you have suffered so, but if you are to survive this experience, you must do as I have said."

"I will," Victor responded.

"If there are any issues, call this number," Jeremy added. "If I do not hear from you, I will assume that no news is good news and I will call as soon as my plane touches down in Logan Airport. Good bye, Victor."

"Good bye," he replied and ended the call.

Victor stood up and got dressed, his exhaustion gone, his tiredness forgotten. He snatched up his wallet, stuffing it into his back pocket as he hurried down the stairs. Grabbing his keys from the hall table, Victor hurried to the side door, ignoring the mocking laughter of the bear as he fled his own house.

Chapter 11: Tensions Rise

Jeremy Rhinehart put his cellphone away and leaned on his cane. Behind him, Chief Carroll of the Litchfield, Connecticut police force waited impatiently. The officer had accompanied Jeremy, albeit unwillingly, into Kent Falls State Park.

"Are you done?" the officer asked, not bothering to hide his disdain for Jeremy.

"I am," Jeremy responded.

The lights of the police SUV shined on the small, covered bridge. Small insects darted in and out of the light beams that illuminated the deep red walls and white trim of the bridge.

"Are you going to stand there all night, or actually do something?" the chief sneered. "You know, you may have convinced the folks in town hall that you know what you're doing, but I know you're running a con. Seen enough of them in my time."

"I'm sure you have, Chief," Jeremy said evenly, "and I can assure you that what you have here isn't a con. I wish it was. My consultation fee is more than my removal fee, and that is simply because too many people don't actually have a paranormal problem. The Kent Park, however, does."

Jeremy glanced over his shoulder at the man. Chief Carroll looked as if he could star in a television program about small town police officers who had once been local football heroes, or baseball stars. A single conversation had been enough for Jeremy, and while he would have preferred to work alone, the board of selectmen had been adamant that he take the chief along.

They had mistaken Jeremy's cane as a sign of infirmity.

"Are you ready, Chief?" Jeremy asked politely.

The man snorted and nodded.

"Pick up the box then, please," Jeremy said, his tone no longer asking, but telling. Commanding the other man to obey.

Carroll seemed to surprise himself at the rapidity with which he followed Jeremy's order.

"God in heaven," the chief muttered, "what do you have in here?"

"As of right now," Jeremy said, leaning on his cane while walking toward the covered bridge, "nothing."

"Well, what is this made of?" Carroll demanded. "Lead?"

"Yes," Jeremy answered, and then he kept his attention focused on the bridge. The insects had slipped away. Beneath them, the creek bed was silent except for the soft noises of the water as it passed under the bridge. The air should have been loud with the cries and calls of frogs, with the howls of night predators seeking their meals. But it wasn't.

There was nothing.

Jeremy moved to where the bridge and the paved road met, his breath suddenly coming out in long, white curls, the temperature plummeting.

"How is this happening?" Carroll hissed. He no longer accused Jeremy.

"Don't think about it," Jeremy commanded. "Focus on the box, Chief. When I tell you to open it, you open it. When I tell you to close it, close it. And when I tell you to lock it, you damned well better lock that safe. Understood?"

"Yes, sir," Carroll whispered, all traces of disdain gone. They had been replaced with fear.

Jeremy stepped onto the bridge and came to a stop. He let his eyes go out of focus, staring at the horizon and nothing more. In silence he waited, knowing it would appear soon enough.

Less than a minute later, it had.

A glimmer on top of a rafter. It looked as though a bit of moonlight had caught a nail head, but Jeremy knew better. The roof was too well done. There were no holes in it to let in the light.

But Jeremy didn't move towards the object. He had read the reports. Some had said there were more than two creatures on the bridge. If it was true, then there might be a second item.

He waited a long time, the chief's breathing becoming louder the longer they stood there.

Finally, after almost ten minutes, the second object flickered. It was beneath the first, near the floor.

Jeremy reached into his pocket, removed a pair of thick, leather gloves, and put them on.

"Follow me, Chief," Jeremy said, and he stepped toward the two objects.

As he did so, one of the spirits appeared.

It was exactly as it had been described. Tall and thin, an emaciated corpse with a death's head grin, all teeth, and split lips. The eyes were sunken in their sockets, and wisps of white hair clung to pale skin. With a shriek of pure glee, it launched itself at Jeremy, who brought his cane up in a graceful arc. The iron covered tip of the cane slashed through the ghost, and its smile of sick pleasure vanished a split second, before the spirit did the same.

Jeremy let the cane continue its upward movement, the tip knocking down the object from the rafter. As he caught it in his free hand the second creature appeared.

It was as foul as the first, yet it was female. Her smile was stretched back to almost her ears, the portrait of a lunatic. She, like her mate, sprang at Jeremy.

Her fate was the same as the first.

Without caution for the frail body, Jeremy bent down and scooped up the second object. He didn't bother looking at them. Instead, he called out, "Chief Carroll, could you open the box, please?"

The chief didn't answer, but Jeremy heard the familiar creak of the hinges.

With a quick spin, Jeremy turned and dropped the items into the box. Before they had struck the bottom, he was slamming the lid down and locking it.

He took a deep, calming breath and smiled up at the chief.

"There," Jeremy said, "all finished."

"What were those things?" Carroll whispered, his voice shuddering.

"Foul," Jeremy replied. "Would you be so kind as to carry the box to my car?"

Carroll nodded, and he didn't speak again until after he had placed the container in the back seat.

"Do you do this a lot?" Carroll asked.

"It is all I do," Jeremy answered.

"Is that how you hurt your hip?" the officer asked.

"That, good sir," Jeremy answered, smiling, "was a mine in Vietnam. Thank you for your assistance this morning, it is much appreciated."

Leaving the man behind, Jeremy got into the car and left the state park. He had a plane to catch, and a murderous toy to investigate.

Chapter 12: The Arrival of Anne

She was in front of his door when he arrived home from the antique store.

Grant's heart skipped a beat as he turned off the car, climbed out and hurried to the package. He left his laptop and notes in the car, his focus on Anne and nothing more.

The seller had placed her in a wooden box, the container stamped with 'Fragile' in large, black letters on each side.

Grant smiled as he sank to his knees and gathered the box into his arms. He held it carefully, as one might hold a newborn child, and opened the door. Quick steps carried him over the threshold, and he went to the security system, typing in the code to turn off the activation of the alarm. He carried the box into the dining room, set it down on the bamboo placemat at his own seat and left her, reluctantly. Grant returned to his car, took out his notes and laptop, and then hurried back to the dining room, locking up behind him.

When he reached the box, he put his belongings on the table and smiled. His hands shook as he turned the container around, found the shipping label and withdrew the packing slip. There was a confirmation number, saying his money had cleared, as well as a note from the seller that wished Grant the best of luck with his new acquisition.

He chuckled, picked up the box, and left the dining room. At the far end of the house was a small room. There was a door which led from the hall into the room, and a second from it into his bedroom. His most prized dolls stood there, protected from UV lights and the harsh rays of the sun in cases designed specifically for the care of delicate antiques.

At that time, only three of the seven cases were occupied, but when the package was opened, Anne would be set in the place of honor, and then only three would be empty.

Grant sat down on the floor with the box. When he had first purchased her, Grant had brought the tools out and put them in the center of the room. They had been waiting for her, just as Grant had.

With steady hands, he pried open the box, the brad-point nails screeching against the wood as he pulled them out.

Curled shavings and packing peanuts were the first objects he saw. His fingers trembled as he plucked out handfuls of the packing material and dropped it to the floor. Soon a small, leather valise was revealed, and a gasp of pleasure escaped his lips.

Grant retrieved it with the skill and grace of a surgeon, opening the small piece of luggage and sighing with joy at the sight of the small, folded clothes within. The sweet smell of violets drifted out, reminding him of his grandmother.

Blinking back tears, Grant placed the valise on the floor and returned his attention to the box. Soon his fingers brushed against fabric and smooth porcelain. He eased her out and held her up in the light. Her features were fine, her color magnificent. The ringlets in her hair had a spring to them, and Grant was amazed.

Anne was worth far more than the two thousand dollars he had spent for her.

He got to his feet and carried her with reverence to her case. She stood easily in the glass confines, her back resting against the clear acrylic brace.

"Hello, Anne," Grant whispered, "I'm so glad you've come to visit."

He closed the case, locked it, and turned back to the mess on the floor. Humming to himself, he cleaned up the packaging material, carried the trash out to the hallway, and went back in for the valise. Beneath the case was a small cabinet, and he placed the luggage within it. There were also small gauges that measured the humidity and temperature in the display case.

Everything looked to be in order, although the internal temperature was at sixty-two degrees when it should have been at a calm and steady seventy.

Grant's stomach rumbled and reminded him that he hadn't eaten since his last appointment or his shopping trip at the antique store. Sixty-two degrees was still well within the safe limits for his newest girl. He would check on her after he had a quick bite, and a glass of celebratory wine.

Grant smiled as he left the room, turned off the light and said, "Good night, Anne."

As the door clicked shut he straightened up, his smile faltering, his hand still on the doorknob.

In the stillness of the room, he had heard a noise.

A voice.

That of a young girl whispering good night to him.

Beneath his hand, the doorknob grew cold, and through the wood of the door, he heard a girl begin to sing in French.

Chapter 13: Afraid and Alone

Victor had passed out from exhaustion and woke well past check out time at the local Howard Johnson's hotel. His body screamed for sustenance, and he obliged, ordering overpriced room service and devouring it, drinking two cups of hot coffee. With the food in his stomach, Victor had shuffled to the bathroom, washed up and prepared for the day.

He gathered up his phone and wallet, checked out of the room and paid the extra day without any argument. Thoughts of lead safes and antique stores occupied his mind. He drove up into Amherst, New Hampshire where a stretch of Route 101 was inundated with antique and consignment shops. After the first stop, which proved uneventful and left him frustrated, Victor picked up another cup of coffee. He hoped the caffeine would help keep him focused, and not leaving him shaking like an addict suffering through withdrawals.

Victor searched through four more stores, and it wasn't until he reached Milford, New Hampshire that he found what Jeremy Rhinehart had recommended. In a small consignment shop called Robin's Egg, he found a child's safe tucked away in a back corner. Whoever had labeled it had added 'Danger, Lead Lined!'

The price was forty-seven dollars and fifty cents, which he thought was a strange and obscure number to choose, but he paid for it. He muddled through the small talk the young woman behind the counter had insisted upon as he waited for his card to be accepted. When she handed him the receipt and wished him a nice day, Victor had to stop himself from running out the door.

Across the street from Robin's Egg was a strip mall which contained a hardware store. Victor stopped there next, purchasing himself a pair of heavy-duty leather working gloves on the off chance that he might come into contact with the bear.

He shuddered at the idea of it, squeezing the gloves in his hands as he hurried back to his car. Driving back to Pepperell was difficult, he wanted to race along the roads, break the speed limit, and send his vehicle hurtling to the house.

A burning bile rose up in his throat as he thought about the bear. He pictured it in the basement, in his library, waiting for him. Eager to mock and remind him of Erin's death.

Soon Victor was on his own street, pulling in once again to the driveway of the house he had once shared with Erin. A house stripped of its title of 'home' by the toy.

Victor found himself sweating, pushing open the side door, and clambering into the kitchen. He stopped and tilted his head, listening.

From the basement door, he heard a shrill laugh, and the bear's voice followed.

"You've come back, Victor," the toy said, mocking him. "I'm surprised. I thought you were a coward."

Fear sprang up, and Victor forced himself to go to the basement door. He pulled on the gloves, wrenched it open, and flicked on the light. He made his way down, step by step, one hand holding the railing, the other cradling the heavy toy safe in his arm.

Victor walked to his library, the bear's voice growing louder.

"What have you brought?" the toy inquired a note of concern in its voice. "There's something foul in your hands. What is it?"

Victor didn't answer it.

"You had better tell me," the bear snarled.

A heavy book went hurtling off a shelf, smashing into Victor's arm. Pain blossomed in the muscle, threatening to force him to drop the safe, but he held onto it, refusing to let go.

"What is that?!" the bear shrieked.

More books flew off the shelves, some only grazing Victor while others crashed into him. He stumbled, but kept his balance. His hatred for the toy kept him moving forward, his eyes fixed on the small bear.

Victor watched as its head swiveled to face him, a malignant gleam in its small eyes.

"Tell me!" the bear screamed, its disembodied voice all around Victor, pummeling at his thoughts.

"No," Victor growled as he surged forward. He flung open the door of the safe and slapped the bear into its lead-lined confines. As he slammed the door shut, and spun the combination to lock it, a final book hurtled off the shelf, pinwheeling into Victor's forehead and knocking him backward.

His knees loosened, and he felt his eyes roll up as he collapsed to the floor, the safe falling out of his hands, and crashing down beside him.

Victor tried to get back to his feet, but he couldn't open his eyes, and his limbs refused to respond. He attempted to regain control of himself once more, then gave up and let unconsciousness and exhaustion drag him into darkness.

Chapter 14: Northfield, Vermont, a Robbery Occurs

Stefan had left his phone at home. He had stolen a 1998 Crown Victoria, then the license plates off another Crown Victoria two hundred miles away. From his emergency supply of cash, he had taken enough money to drive up to Northfield and back. On the way there, he had stopped at an indoor flea market in New Hampshire and purchased a cheap survival knife of a style made famous by the *Rambo* movies. It was untraceable and would be effective.

He had wiped the weapon down a dozen times since he had purchased it, and he knew he would do so another ten times at least. Stefan was well aware of his own obsessive behaviors.

They had kept him alive far longer than anyone had expected.

He planned to remain alive and to exact vengeance on his mother's memory and those who shared her passion for the dead. Long before she had died, Stefan decided he would punish all like her and his father. Those who would sacrifice time, money, and effort on the dead, who had been foolish enough to bind themselves to some paltry item.

As he grew older, and became wiser, Stefan learned that it was best to stop problems before they started. There was a reason why, in certain situations, anyone over the age of ten had to be put down, and Stefan had never had an issue pulling the trigger. Selling his mother's haunted items to amateurs would serve two purposes. The first would be the dispersal of what she had prized above him. The second would kill or maim those he sold the pieces to.

And after that, Stefan knew, he could focus on those older collectors. Men and women like his parents.

Like Collier.

Mr. Aldo Collier had proven himself a nuisance, and his continued interruptions would inhibit Stefan's plans. It was a situation he found untenable, and he needed to stop it before Collier interfered again. While he would have preferred to have killed the man in a far more excruciating and fitting manner, a quick death was necessary if Stefan was going to be able to see all of his plans come to fruition.

Stefan was a short distance from the campus of Norwich University, his car parked in the driveway of an abandoned house. He was not with the car.

Instead, Stefan was on East Street in downtown Northfield. He hid on a set of stairs that descended to a sublevel business, which lacked any sort of security cameras. From where he stood, Stefan could see the Good Measure Brewing Company, where Aldo Collier was enjoying his nightly beer. The man's gaudy Lexus was parked up the street, and Collier would need to pass by Stefan's hiding place to get to his vehicle.

Collier, like so many people, was a creature of habit. As a single man, he ate breakfast at a local diner. Had lunch in the same, and then dinner at the Good Measure. He would stay there from six in the evening until nine at night. Collier was punctual and did not vary from his established pattern.

It was the only trait Stefan appreciated.

Stefan didn't worry about checking the time or looking for people out for a late evening walk. A few scattered individuals were to be found, but they were victims of the Northeast's heroin epidemic, more concerned with scoring their next fix than what was going on in the world around them.

Stefan had taken the precaution of paying a local dealer to give out freebies to the junkies, thus keeping them occupied for the evening.

That same dealer's body was rotting in a dumpster, the money back in Stefan's pocket.

Stefan disliked unnecessary risks.

He heard the door of the Good Measure open and his eyes locked on it. Aldo stepped out, the dull street lights illuminating the garish pink suit and mauve shirt he wore. On the sidewalk, Collier stepped away from the door, took out his phone, and dialed a number. His one sided conversation was audible from Stefan's position.

Collier frowned as he spoke.

"Mr. Korzh, I'm beginning to suspect that you are avoiding me, sir," Collier said to Stefan's voicemail. "I can assure you that I will not stop calling. You have my number, sir. I look forward to hearing from you."

Collier shook his head, put the phone away, and stepped off the curb without any concern for traffic. Stefan didn't blame him. He had seen one car pass by in the hour and a half since he had taken up a seat on the stairs. He whistled a nameless tune, disappearing from Stefan's view for a moment when he reached the opposite side of East Street. The whistling continued unabated, and a heartbeat later he reappeared, walking towards Stefan's position. When Collier came abreast of him, Stefan's left arm shot out, grabbed hold of the other man's thick ankle and jerked his leg out from underneath him.

Collier let out a short scream of surprise, but it was cut short as the man's face smashed into the sidewalk. Stefan sprang out, knife in hand. He straddled Collier, whose pitiful groans and mewling sounds filled the air, and drove the weapon into the man's back. As the spinal column was severed, Stefan ripped Collier's phone and wallet out of their pockets, stripped off the man's watch and cut off the man's ring finger. He twisted a large, diamond-studded band from the bleeding finger and tossed the meat to the pavement.

"Oh my God!"

Stefan's head snapped up, and he saw a young woman, her eyes wide in shock and horror. He leaped forward and drove the knife blade deep enough into her chest that the sternum cracked from the pressure. She fell backward, taking the weapon with her. Stefan ground his teeth in rage at the disruption of his plan, placed a foot on her chest and yanked the knife free with a harsh twist.

A quick slash severed her purse strap, and he took it with him as he vanished up a side street.

Behind him, two people lay dying, and the future looked bright.

Chapter 15: A Strange Conversation

When Victor had awoken, he had been relieved to discover the bear had not only still been in the safe, but that Victor couldn't hear the wretched toy.

He had left the safe in the library and gone upstairs to call Jeremy Rhinehart. The other man had called him back a few hours later, saying he had landed at the airport and asking for directions.

Victor had given them with a sense of relief, and he waited in the kitchen for Jeremy to arrive.

Several hours later, there was a knock at the door, and when Victor answered it, he found Jeremy Rhinehart.

The man was rather ordinary. He was neither too tall nor was he too short. Jeremy looked to be somewhere in his late sixties or early seventies, and he leaned on a cane made of black steel. His features were bland, his hair a soft brown with wide swaths of gray at the temples. The only aspect of Jeremy that stood out were his eyes. They were the deepest blue Victor had ever seen. It was almost as if they weren't made of flesh and blood, but something ethereal and altogether unnatural.

"Hello, I'm Jeremy Rhinehart," the man said, extending a hand, "we spoke on the phone."

"Yes, yes we did," Victor replied, a note of apology in his tone. "Please, come in."

As he backed away from the door, he noticed Jeremy's cane and how each step seemed to pain the man.

"Can I get you anything to eat or drink?" Victor asked, closing and locking the door.

"No, thank you," Jeremy said, smiling. "I ate at the airport before I came here. And I had coffee as well. I had some rather late nights, and I'm still trying to recuperate from the loss of sleep. I'm not a young man anymore."

"Did you have a good flight?" Victor asked, leading the way into the kitchen.

"Yes, it was," Jeremy answered, sitting down at the table. "Both there and back, thankfully. But let us get down to the heart of the matter here. You say you have a haunted toy?"

Victor nodded. "Downstairs. I got a safe like you said. And I didn't touch it. The damned thing was pretty upset though. It was throwing books at me the whole time."

Jeremy raised an eyebrow as he sat back.

"And this is the toy you said convinced your wife to kill herself?" the man asked.

Victor nodded, unable to speak.

"May I ask you for a favor, Victor?" Jeremy asked in a soft voice.

"Sure," Victor managed to say.

"Would you be so kind as to go down stairs and retrieve the safe for me?" Jeremy said.

Victor felt a bolt of fear slash through him, but he swallowed his anxiety back and replied, "Yes, I can do that."

He took a deep breath, got up from his seat and passed by the older man as he fixed his eyes on the basement door. Victor knew he had the bear trapped in the safe, but there was a gnawing bit of worry that it had found a way out, that it was waiting for him.

Victor fought back the fear and opened the basement door.

The sound of each footstep on the stairs was too loud. Every creak magnified, the shadows darker than they should have been.

Victor's breath came in short, sharp draws, painful and difficult for his lungs to process. His eyes locked onto the safe and his steps faltered. He forced himself forward, fearing that the bear's voice would creep out of the lead-lined box and assault him. Afraid that he wouldn't be able to avenge Erin's death.

Yet no voice issued forth. No books flew off the shelves to join the others that still lay on the floor.

Victor reached out, picked up the safe, the metal cool beneath his hands, and carried it upstairs to the kitchen table. He set it down in front of Jeremy and took a nervous step back.

Jeremy smiled his thanks and said, "I wonder Victor, would you trust me to be alone in your home for a short time?"

"Um, sure," Victor answered. "How long do you need me to leave?"

"If you would like to step outside," Jeremy said, "perhaps do a bit of yard work or take a walk around the block, it shouldn't take too long. Should the bear prove to be more difficult than I am prepared for, then I shall close the safe back up and plan for another avenue of attack."

"Okay," Victor said, "I'll step outside, just sit in my car. If you want you can wave out the door to me, or call me on my phone."

"I'll call you," Jeremy said, smiling. "May I have the combination?"

"Sure, 4-6-5," he said.

"Thank you," Jeremy said, and Victor gave a nod and left the old man sitting in front of the small safe.

Chapter 16: Speaking with the Bear

Jeremy reached into his pocket and pulled out a pair of white cotton gloves. He slipped them on and spun the combination lock to clear it. Then, with a deep breath, Jeremy entered the combination, heard the tumblers click, and opened the safe.

A small, brown toy bear sat upright. It was old, the kind of toy that was wound by a key. Jeremy had owned one as a child, and he remembered how it had tumbled over and over and across the wooden floor.

From the safe, a cold draft emerged, and Jeremy sat back in the chair, crossing his arms over his chest.

"Hello," he said.

The bear didn't respond.

"I have a finite amount of time here," Jeremy continued, "and you can either speak with me, or I can close the door and lock you back in."

Out of the corner of his eye, Jeremy saw a cup lift up off the counter top.

Frowning, he reached out and closed the safe.

The cup slammed back down, spinning crazily on one side until it went tumbling onto the floor, where it shattered on the tile.

Jeremy counted to twenty and opened the safe.

"I hate you," the bear hissed, its voice dark and full of spite.

"I'm sure you do. I'm not particularly fond of you right now either," Jeremy said. "Now, let's start from the beginning, shall we?"

The bear didn't respond.

"My name is Jeremy Rhinehart," he said, "what is yours?"

"I know your name," the bear grumbled. "I won't give you mine."

Jeremy stretched his hand out to the door, and the bear snapped, "Rolf!"

"Rolf?" Jeremy asked, returning his hand to his lap. "Well, it is a pleasure to meet you, Rolf. Now, where did you come from?"

The ghost went into a long and filthy tirade about reproduction.

Jeremy waited until Rolf had finished and said, "Excellent. Now, when did you die? And, before you say anything you'll regret, I want to tell you that I am running low on patience."

For a moment, there was no response from Rolf, then a deep, cruel chuckle escaped from the safe.

"When did I die, Jeremy?" the bear asked. "When your grandfather was still a boy in Berlin. When we were still starving after the war and packing our bread with sawdust to thicken the loaves. I knew famine and war and hatred. I remember what the British did, and when I thought of that time, I showed her death."

The hint of a memory struggled to rise in Jeremy's mind, but he couldn't focus.

"I don't believe you," Jeremy said.

Rolf snorted. "Believe me, don't believe me. I don't care. You're going to die. He's going to die. All of you are going to die. It's one truth we cannot escape. Would you not prefer to do it now?"

"Not particularly," Jeremy replied.

A groan sounded behind Rolf, and he twisted around in time to see the refrigerator falling towards him.

With a desperate lunge, he threw himself out of the chair and onto the floor, landing hard on his bad hip. Pain shot up through his side as the appliance crashed to the floor. The muffled sound of glass breaking mingled with Rolf's high-pitched laughter.

"Oh, to kill you," Rolf brayed, "what a glorious feat that would be. Do you think you are unknown, Jailer? We know of you. We all know of you, and we all seek your death. She's dead now, and he'll free us, one by one. Set us after you, and we will hunt you down like the dog you are."

The cabinet doors thundered open, and dishes flew off their shelves. Jeremy protected his face with an upraised arm and managed to climb to his feet. Shards of broken plates and bowls and cups formed a whirlwind around him, the sharp edges slashing at his face and hands.

With a snarl, Jeremy staggered forward, grabbed the safe's door, and slammed it shut.

The airborne items plummeted to the floor while Jeremy leaned against the table for support. Around him, the kitchen was a chaotic mess, and the possessed toy bear was imprisoned once again in the safe. A strange sense of fear settled into the base of his neck as Jeremy reflected on what Rolf had said.

The fear grew as the memory which had remained hidden finally emerged.

Jeremy had heard of a toy bear inhabited by a killer before. And that toy bear had been part of a collection. A much larger collection owned by Nicole Korzh, a woman who had amassed a horrifying amount of dangerous, possessed items.

And she's dead, Jeremy thought, *and someone is setting them free in the world.*

He stared at the safe and wondered how much damage the unknown seller had caused.

Chapter 17: Learning the Truth

Each night, Anne sang a beautiful, sweet song in French.

At first, there had been a touch of fear, the idea that he truly owned a possessed doll. The trepidation had quickly been replaced by a sense of pride. After all his years of collecting, Grant finally owned a haunted item. It was almost a badge of honor in New Orleans, and he bragged about it to several of his friends.

His pride became mixed with curiosity when he bothered to record Anne's song and couldn't find a translation of it.

It took him several hours to realize it was sung in a patois that he was unfamiliar with, but he decided to take it with him into the French Quarter to see if there was anyone who could translate her song.

He had found such a person in Leanne Le Monde. She was an elderly lady and had been referred to him by almost everyone Grant had spoken with in his search.

Grant waited in her sitting room with a glass of tea spiked with cognac. It was a heady mixture he enjoyed as the warmth of the room wrapped around him and lulled him into a pleasant daze. He was nearly asleep when the door to her private office opened, and she stepped out.

Leanne Le Monde was a large woman, both in height and girth. Her skin was dark, and a sense of power emanated from her.

Grant got to his feet and saw she was at least six inches taller than he was.

"Hello," he said, setting the glass down on the coffee table and giving a short bow.

"Hello yourself," she said, her voice smooth and elegant. There was a hint of a Parisian accent in her words and Grant knew he wouldn't be surprised if she had been educated in France.

"You have brought me something to listen to, yes?" she asked, motioning for him to follow her into the office.

"Yes, Ms. Le Monde," he said, waiting for her to sit down before he did so.

She smiled. "It is Mrs. Le Monde, although Henri passed away almost thirty years ago. Now tell me, before I listen, where it is you made this recording."

He quickly explained to her about his collection and his recent acquisition of Anne.

Leanne did not seem to admire his sense of pride. Her eyes narrowed, and she asked, "You have allowed this creature to remain in your home?"

"Yes," Grant said, feeling confused, "why wouldn't I?"

"The dead may be with us," she said, "but they do not belong with us. They should not be coddled. To do so only invites trouble, young man, and I suspect that is what you have brought into your house. They are like children. Spoiled children. Except these will kill you, and they will feel no remorse for it."

Grant wanted to argue with her and state that he didn't believe ghosts could hurt someone, but the expression on Leanne's face and the fierceness in her voice suggested he remain silent.

She shook her head and said, "Play this doll's song for me, young man, and pray that she is not like the others I have known."

Grant cleared his throat, nodded, and withdrew the small electronic voice recorder he had purchased. He pressed play and held it up for Leanne to listen to.

As Anne's beautiful voice filled the room, the old woman's face grew hard, the line of her jaw setting into place firmly. She remained silent until Anne's song finished.

"It is indeed an old patois," Leanne said after several minutes of silence. "One that has not been heard in the South for a very long time. And then, it was last heard on the islands off the Carolinas."

She hesitated, and Grant waited for her to continue.

Before she did, Leanne stood up and walked over to a large bar. She fixed herself a drink and carried it back to the chair. The ice in the glass clinked, and Grant couldn't tell if it was from fear or palsy.

"You need to send the doll back to whomever you purchased it from," she said.

Grant looked at her, confused. "Why would I do something like that?"

"You really have no idea what she is saying, do you?" Leanne mused.

"No," Grant said, "I don't."

Leanne closed her eyes and wrapped both hands around her glass. The ice cubes ceased their rattling. She was quiet for a long time. Long enough that Grant had decided she had either fallen asleep or died when suddenly he found her staring at him.

"Listen closely, young man," Leanne said, and there was no trace of infirmity or age in her voice. "That doll in your house is death. She has killed before, and she seeks to kill again. When she learns your name, you will hear it, for she will sing it morning, noon, and night. Find the seller, return it to them, and do not take it back."

Grant swallowed nervously, rubbed at the back of his neck and asked in a voice that cracked with tension, "What is she saying in her song?"

Leanne leaned forward, her eyes locked onto his and whispered, "In their sleep, I strangled them, babes and husband and kin. In their sleep, I stitched their eyes with thread so fine and thin."

Chapter 18: At the Diner

Jeremy's face, arms, and hands were a patchwork of Band-Aids and bandages. The older man would have looked funny if he hadn't almost died at Rolf's hands.

Victor nodded his thanks to the waitress who brought them their coffee. He was surprised his hands didn't shake as he emptied four packets of sugar and cream each into the thick, porcelain mug. The metal spoon was heavy and ungainly in his hand, the oversized head bouncing along the interior of the mug.

"Are you alright?" Jeremy asked.

"Hm?" Victor said, then nodded. "Yeah. Yes. I don't know. I'm confused. I didn't believe in ghosts. I didn't think they were real. I always thought it was some silly hobby of Erin's, gathering up stuff people told her was haunted."

"The bear," Jeremy said, "is not merely haunted. It is possessed. There is a longer, darker story behind it than most, and I intend to ferret it out. I am concerned for you, Victor. What are your plans? Will you stay in that house?"

Victor nodded. "For now, at least. I'll put it up for sale, and when it's sold, I'll move. I can't afford to do so otherwise."

Jeremy rubbed at his chin, hit a cut, and winced. "What do you do for work, if you don't mind my asking?"

"I'm an independent researcher," Victor said, pleased to have the conversation move away from ghosts. "I'm working on some Revolutionary War material for a 'Daughters of the American Revolution' chapter down in Maryland."

"I think," Jeremy said, "that I could use your help if you would be willing."

Victor put the spoon down on his plate and asked, "What type of help?"

"The story behind Rolf," Jeremy said. "I am not nearly as adept at using a computer as most people, and I am afraid that I find libraries rather frightening."

Victor could not stop the expression of astonishment that appeared.

Jeremy smiled ruefully, nodding. "It's true. The first haunted item I came into contact with as a boy was in a library. It was a book, and yes, it was actually haunted by an old librarian. Let me sum it up by saying she was not a fan of children. I have not felt comfortable in a library since."

The idea of a book being haunted caused Victor to wince, but he pushed the idea to the back of his mind as he said, "I'd love to work with you. Where do you live?"

"Presently, I have an apartment in Boston," Jeremy said, "but I do own a large home in Norwich, Connecticut. I keep my gathered items there, under lock and key. I tend to travel a bit, and there are two bedrooms in the Boston residence. Should you sell your house you are more than welcome to reside with me until you find a permanent place to rest your head."

"That sounds great," Victor said, straightening up.

"I'm glad," Jeremy said. He smiled and added, "Now I must caution you. In the quest for the seller of Rolf, I cannot stress the danger that you would be in. Anyone that could control a spirit as powerful as Rolf for any amount of time has to be strong. In addition to that, the seller will not want to be found. They will do whatever is necessary to keep that from happening. I suspect that violence would be an option they favored."

"So I can't confront this guy if I find him? Or her?" Victor asked, frowning.

"You certainly cannot," Jeremy said, and there was a harsh note in his voice. "Nothing is going to be as it seems now, Victor. You're going to enter a world you had no idea existed, and at times, you'll find it is a terrible and dark place. The horrors you can stumble upon here are nothing compared to what you know of now, and even the mundane in this new world will be terrifying to the life you are leaving behind. Will you trust me on this?"

"Yes," Victor said, hesitating only for a moment. "I will."

"Good," Jeremy said, sighing. "Now, let's drink our coffee, and I'll tell you how to take hold of the dead."

Chapter 19: Afraid to Go Home

Grant had wandered around the French Quarter for hours before he eventually called on a friend and met him for drinks. After that, Grant had gone to a hotel, checking in for the night. The idea of returning to his apartment left him sickened. The stark, brutal realization that the doll truly was haunted, and that it was murderous as well, had stripped him of his cavalier attitude. And since Leanne had translated only part of the song for him, Grant guessed that it only got worse.

Once in the hotel room, he had committed the cardinal sin of opening the minibar, but he felt every drop of overpriced alcohol was worth it. He sat at the desk in the room, wearing only his pants and staring at his laptop. The Etsy website was up on the screen, and he was scrolling through his history, searching for the email exchanges between himself and the seller.

They were there, but there was a message as well.

NA Sante was no longer a registered seller.

No information about NA Sante was available.

Etsy respected the privacy of all who used its website and would gladly cooperate with any legal investigation, should the appropriate documents and court orders be provided.

Grant sagged in his chair, picked up a small, single serving of vodka and drank it, wincing at the bitterness of the alcohol, and wondering if there was truly anything worse than Grey Goose Vodka.

Grant tossed the plastic bottle toward the wastebasket by the desk and missed it by a foot. He shrugged, rubbed his eyes, glanced at the time, and saw it was four in the morning.

Grant forced himself to think, to remember how he had found the seller to begin with. The unknown individual had misspelled bisque and had specialized, it seemed, in haunted items.

Grant straightened up, navigated away from the legal page on Etsy and went into its search engine. He typed in 'bisgue,' and received nothing in return for his troubles.

Deleting the word, Grant searched for 'haunted doll.' Over a hundred items came up, and he read through them all, looking for some sort of similarity to the original posting.

He found nothing.

Grant closed his eyes and forced himself to remember the exact wording of the listing.

Extremely Active!

His eyes snapped open, and he typed the words into the search bar.

Eight items appeared.

All from the same seller, someone named Nan East.

Grant thought the name was odd. It didn't feel right to him, then, with his mind slogging through the haze of vodka, he rearranged the letters.

NA Sante.

Grant had no idea what the letters meant to the seller, but he was certain he had found the person. A happy, relieved feeling surged through him.

I'll order another item, Grant thought, examining the pieces for sale. *Get a return address since I threw everything else out. Yes, all I need is a return address, and I can send it back to them. I don't need the money. No. Not at all.*

The seventh item for sale was a small, Wedgwood teapot. It was scaled for a doll such as Anne, and as he read the description, he smiled.

This delightful piece belonged to an elderly woman. She was adamant that the Wedgwood harbored the spirit of a younger woman, and boy was she right! I've seen this little number jump right off the shelf and land on the floor without breaking. Considering its provenance, its status as a piece of Wedgwood, the fact that it was made for a doll and it's haunted, you're getting a deal at $300!

Grant drunkenly agreed with the seller and purchased the item. He filled in all his information and didn't make any reference to the previous sale under the seller's other pseudonym.

With everything sent in, Grant shut down the computer and had another drink to celebrate the future return of Anne to her previous owner.

The second bottle of vodka ended up on the floor near the first, and Grant managed to get up and fall into bed instead of next to it.

Pleasant, drunken dreams of a home free of ghosts occupied his mind as dawn crept over the horizon.

Chapter 20: Looking for a Score

Sue Jeffries scratched at her arm, that golden spot in the crook between her forearm and her bicep. Beneath the sleeve of her hooded sweatshirt, the particular part of her own skin she was concerned with itched. It did so because the needle marks were healing and there were scabs. More than a few.

And Sue needed to score.

She had gone far too long without her fix, and she was starting to get sick. Her stomach threatened to revolt and pitch her into the bushes, dry heaving and praying to die, but at the same time, she knew she needed to eat. If she didn't, Sue wouldn't have the strength to make enough money to get her heroin. There was also the risk that when she did eat, whatever she managed to force down her throat would be so rotten as to make her vomit or knock her down with cramps.

But she needed a fix.

Sue made her way along the back of a strip mall, spotted a diner, and headed for it. She considered a trip into the diner, sometimes she could convince a manager to give her a meal for free. Her decision was made for her when she saw a police SUV parked out front.

No cop would let her scam a meal. She would be lucky if they didn't pick her up for vagrancy and bring her in. Or, worse, drop her off at the shelter.

Frowning, she changed direction and went to the back of the diner. A smile replaced the frown when she saw the restaurant's dumpster wasn't locked. Amid the smells of rank trash and rotting food, came the smell of potatoes. Those would be good for days.

She made her way around some parked cars and then stopped. Glancing around, she took several furtive steps back, looking down into the interior of an off-white sedan. On the front passenger seat, half-hidden by a navy blue jacket, was a safe.

It wasn't even a real safe, such as someone might have in their house. No, Sue saw it was a child's toy, something for them to think their money was protected in.

When she had been little, her grandfather had given her one. It had belonged to her aunt. He thought Sue could have fun with it since she was always trying to break into locked rooms and drawers. Her aunt had forgotten the combination, and her grandfather had never known it.

It had taken Sue three days to figure out the combination, but she had done it.

And looking into the car, she knew she could do it again.

She didn't know if it was worth breaking the window for.

Then she saw the doors were unlocked.

Her heartbeat raced, and she couldn't believe her luck.

Pulling the sleeve of her sweatshirt down over her hand to make sure she didn't leave any fingerprints, Sue opened the door. She didn't do it slowly, or glance around, knowing that both acts would only draw attention to her. The hinges were well oiled, and she reached in and picked up the safe, closing the door with her hip.

She ignored the weight of the safe and walked to the dumpster, ducking behind it. Her hunger was forgotten as she set the safe down and she got on her belly. Sue put her ear to the cold metal beside the lock, and she spun the dial three times to clear it. Sue then carefully began to turn it, listening for the tell-tale click of the first tumbler.

Chapter 21: Foolishness Repaid

Victor and Jeremy left the diner together, the older man walking slower and leaning on his cane. In silence, Victor adjusted his stride to match Jeremy's. They walked around the side of the building to the rear parking lot. Jeremy's car was older, a sedan, and it had seen better days. Victor harbored a suspicion that the man could afford a better vehicle, but he kept the belief to himself.

Once at the car, Victor stopped by the passenger's side door and waited.

"You can climb in," Jeremy said, getting into the vehicle. "I never lock it. There's never anything to steal."

Victor shook his head at the absurdity of such a thought, but he opened the door. When he did so, he noticed that his jacket, which he had left over the safe, was on the floor.

The safe was gone.

Victor's head snapped up, and he saw an expression of fury on Jeremy's face.

"Who," the older man hissed, "would be so stupid as to steal that safe? It was a child's plaything! Nothing more!"

Victor didn't have an answer. All he could do was shake his head. There were no words for the disappointment and anger he felt. He turned away from Jeremy's car and squeezed his hands into fists, holding back the growing rage.

"We have to find it," Jeremy said, a hard note entering his voice. "If the thief opens it then they will undoubtedly come to harm."

"I don't care about that!" Victor snapped. "That damned ghost killed Erin! I wanted it destroyed!"

"They can't be destroyed," Jeremy said, fixing a firm gaze on Victor, "you need to know that. The best I am able to do is to keep them imprisoned. I haven't met anyone I trust enough to attempt to cast them out of their homes and send them on to the next life. There is the real risk of the ghost being cast adrift, exorcized from something like a bear to find a second item to fester within."

"Well, what are we supposed to do?" Victor demanded.

"Hunt him down," Jeremy said, shaking his head. "We have to wait until something happens."

"Like what?" Victor asked, afraid of the other man's response.

Jeremy looked at him, his mouth set in a grim line as he answered, "Another death."

Chapter 22: Sue and Her Friend

Sue heard yelling in the parking lot, but it was in the back of her mind. Even her body's warring desires for food and heroin had faded. All she focused on was the safe. In the protection offered by the dumpster and the tall grass, she had managed to find and trip two of the tumblers. Her eyes were half closed, ear pressed to the still cold metal as she listened to the gentle clicks.

Then a louder sound filled her ear, that of the final tumbler falling into place and a smile spread across her face. She pulled her ear away, turned the small handle, and opened the door.

Sue was simultaneously disappointed and curious.

The safe was occupied by a toy bear, its brown fur stiff, and its black eyes bright. The arms hung at straight angles away from the body, the legs too.

She reached in, wrapped her hand around the cold toy, and took it out into the day light. A soft voice seemed to whisper in her ear.

"Hello," the voice said, the tone gentle and soothing.

"Hey," she whispered, sitting back and resting a shoulder against the dumpster. She couldn't tell if she was hearing the voice because she was jonesing for a fix, hungry, or just exhausted. Or if it was a combination of all three.

But it was interesting as hell.

"What's your name?" the voice asked.

"Sue," she answered. "What's yours?"

"A special name, would you like to hear?" the voice asked in response.

Sue frowned, slightly confused at the question, but she answered it nonetheless. "Yes, what is it?"

"My name is Rolf," the voice said.

"Are you the bear?" she asked.

"No," Rolf said, chuckling, "the bear is me."

Sue grinned. "Cool."

"What would you like to do, Sue?" Rolf asked.

"I'm hungry," she replied, "and I need my medicine."

"Ah," Rolf said in a knowing tone, "which shall we get first?"

"Food," she said, "or I won't be able to get the medicine."

"Were you going to eat from the trash?" Rolf inquired.

Sue nodded, tears stung her eyes, and she looked away from the bear in shame.

"Shh," Rolf said, "you have no need to be ashamed. I ate a great deal worse than trash. But there is another way. The cook, in the diner. He is at the back door, yes?"

Sue twisted and peered around the edge of the dumpster. She saw a pair of men by the car the safe had been in, and at the diner's kitchen door, she saw the chef. He was a middle-aged man with a beer belly, smoking a cigarette and drinking from a travel mug.

"He's a drunk," Rolf said in a soft voice, "and he is drunk right now. You should talk to him when there is no one there. He will give you food."

"How do you know?" Sue asked, ducking back behind the dumpster.

"He will be sympathetic to your plight," Rolf purred, "trust me, my new friend."

Sue nodded. Her stomach twisted and cramped, and the sound of a car engine filled the back lot. A moment later, the crunch of tires on the asphalt reached her ears, and she peeked out again. The off-white car exited the parking lot, the men were gone and no one was left except the chef in the back of the diner. Without hesitation, Sue got to her feet and hurried across to him.

He was a tired looking man with pale skin and cheeks that sagged. Dark circles from sleepless nights hung beneath his eyes, and his nose was large and swollen, the burst capillaries making it look more like a map than a part of his face.

The chef turned his face towards her and when he did, Sue saw a shift in his eyes. She watched as the irises changed from dull brown to brilliant green and a smile creased the man's unshaven cheeks.

"You're hungry," the man said in a deep voice.

Sue nodded, shocked by the shift in color she had witnessed.

"Stay here," the chef said. He took a final drag off the cigarette and then flicked it out into the parking lot.

She watched him step back into the kitchen. Voices were raised for a moment, one person yelling and another responding at the same volume.

He reappeared a minute later with a large Styrofoam container. The enticing smell of bacon and eggs and home fries wafted out, and Sue found herself salivating.

The man handed her the food and Sue accepted it. As she started to turn away, he asked, "Do you need money?"

Sue was too stunned to do anything other than nod.

He reached into his back pocket and took out his wallet. It was battered and worn, the black leather faded to almost gray. His hands opened it deftly, and he removed all of the cash from it. These he folded and gave to her.

Sue held onto the money with one hand, and the food with the other.

"Go now," the chef said, an unpleasant grin spreading across his face, "and do no right."

Before he could change his mind about the food and money, Sue left the back of the diner.

In her hands, the food was warm, and the bear was cold. Her arm started to itch, but Sue wasn't worried. After she ate, she would score a fix, and as she made her way down the back of the strip mall, she heard a song. It took her only a moment to realize it was Rolf, and the thought of the bear singing made her happy.

Collecting Death

Chapter 23: Paranoia Sets In

Stefan sat at the table in his house. In the rooms around him, the dead muttered and complained. His father's ghosts were silent, a status Stefan had learned to fear as a young child, and to be wary of as an adult.

He had taken the precaution of locking the door and checking the seals, but there was always the possibility one or more of them might get out. They were exceptionally able to adapt, which was why his father had collected them in the first place.

Stefan shook the thoughts of those ghosts away.

He was allowing himself to be distracted from the real reason he was concerned.

The man, Grant, in Louisiana had purchased another item from Etsy. Most times it would not have been an issue, except Stefan had taken the precaution of changing his name, the size of the items being sold, and their theoretical places of origin.

It was a process he had used for years with items of lesser power, and not once had he sold two pieces to one person under separate aliases.

Which meant Stefan had slipped up.

An error on his part could result in a slew of repercussions, none of which would be enjoyable, and any one of them could send him to prison.

Stefan scratched the bridge of his nose and looked at his laptop.

He had a suspicion that Grant might attempt to find him.

For several minutes, Stefan sat in silence before he came to a decision.

He would honor the sale of the Wedgwood teapot, and he would make sure to include a true return address. For the home in Commack, Long Island off the New York coast, a place where he could prepare a trap for the buyer.

It would require a trip, of course, and he might be tracked down by some of the other collectors, but it was a risk he would have to take.

Stefan nodded to himself, took up a notepad, and jotted down a list of items he would need for the ambush of the

63

buyer. With that finished, he confirmed the sale of the teapot and then searched for news in New England.

The murders of Aldo Collier and a woman named Rebecca Furlong in the small town of Northfield, Vermont dominated the news. He scrolled through the obituaries of several northern Massachusetts towns and found one for Erin Daniels, who died suddenly in her home.

Stefan smirked, a sense of satisfaction settling over him. One by one, he would punish those who sought to collect the dead as his parents had.

The smugness he felt had faded away as he thought of the buyer in Louisiana. That man was still alive, and Anne was not known for her subtle nature.

He scratched at the bridge of his nose for a moment, then stood up and left the dining room. Angry growls and hisses filled the air, and he cursed them into silence, threatening them with lead coffins as he stomped up the stairs. At the end of the hall stood the door to the room that held all of his father's ghosts.

And his father's as well.

As he thought of his father, the man's voice tore through the house.

"Stefanushka!" the man called and Stefan winced.

He wanted to retreat to his bedroom but he knew if he didn't answer his father's summons there would be no peace in the house. Without quiet he wouldn't be able to sleep, and without sleep there would be no vengeance against his parents.

Frowning, Stefan walked to the door and examined the seals with a cautious eye. It was never wise to let down his guard around them.

"Yes," Stefan grumbled.

The sound of his own voice seemed to cause a disturbance among his father's ghosts as a rolling rumble made itself known, and Stefan shivered. Voices speaking Vietnamese and Pashto, Chinese and English, mingled together and Stefan took a nervous step back.

"Stay here, Stefanushka," his father said, the sound of his voice coming from close to the top of the door, mimicking the height of Ivan Korzh in life.

"Why?" Stefan asked, then flinched as the door rattled in its frame, and his father yelled in Pashto. A freezing blast of air sent Stefan staggering back. The walls of the house shook to its foundation. Glasses crashed in the kitchen, and a piece of furniture fell over in the sitting room.

The battle behind the door lasted for several minutes, allowing Stefan time to regain his balance. He prepared to flee to the first floor, but he hesitated. It would not do well to ask his father a question and then leave. The man had as little patience dead as he had when alive.

"Are you still there, Stefanushka?" his father asked, a chuckle rippling through the question.

"Yes," Stefan answered, keeping his irritation in check.

"Excellent," Ivan said, "now, I have a question for you."

"You do?" Stefan asked in reply, suddenly wary.

"Why, Stefanushka, are you selling your mother's items?" The anger and disdain in his father's voice was clear through the door and the protective seals.

"What?" Stefan demanded. "Why would you think that?"

"Do not be stupid," his father snapped, and Stefan recoiled as though his father had reached through the door and struck him. "And watch your tone!"

Stefan bit back his anger and said in a forced, even tenor, "I'm doing what I have to do. That's all."

"Listen to me, Stefan," Ivan said, dropping the familial nickname, "I know what you are doing, and you must stop this nonsense. Your mother and I spent our lives seeking the dead out and gathering them here. Do you not understand that others will trace the dead back to you?"

"No," Stefan answered. "They can't."

"Fool!" his father screamed. "They can!"

"You don't know what you're talking about," Stefan muttered, and a harsh blow struck him on the side of the head.

He clapped a hand to the injured spot as he let out a yelp.

A painful silence descended on the hall.

"There is a man," Ivan stated in a cold tone, "who will find you. A man will hound you. We can feel it. And he is not the only one."

Stefan looked sharply at the door.

"What the hell do you mean?" he demanded. "None of the other collectors know where I am right now. And I took care of the one who had found me."

His father snorted. "This other man in Massachusetts is not a collector, although he is assisted by one. No, I have learned that you sent Rolf to her, and thus you murdered his wife by doing so. You are being foolish, Stefanushka, and you will find yourself here sooner rather than later."

Stefan managed not to flinch at the thought of an eternity spent with his father and the man's ghosts.

"Now," Ivan said dismissively, "You will stop selling your mother's prizes. You will retrieve those you have sent back into the wild. And understand this, if you fail I will make certain you will join me, and remember, Stefanushka, you will not do well here amongst my dead."

"Sure," Stefan muttered, hiding his hate for the man as he hurried away from the door. His mind raced with plans of taking care of Grant and an uncomfortable worry pulsed in the back of his thoughts.

His father's ghosts were the stuff of nightmares.

Chapter 24: Back at Victor's House

Victor had cleaned up the broken glass and shattered dishes. The house was no longer cold from Rolf, but it was still lifeless, the heart ripped out of it.

Two days had passed since the theft of the safe, and Jeremy had come back earlier from Boston. The man was in the spare bedroom, returning calls and answering emails. Soon they would go out into town and search again for some sign of the bear. Of any hint of who might have taken it, and why.

Victor walked across the dining room, and stood at the windows that looked out over the front yard. Across the street, he saw someone standing next to Alfred Case's house.

It was a young woman, half in the shadows, staring at Victor's house.

He felt uneasy as he watched her.

The woman shifted, and he saw that she wore a hooded sweatshirt. It was a dirty gray, and her jeans were torn. Her clothes hung on her loosely, and what might have once been a pretty face was thin and haggard. The young woman's lips were pressed into a thin line and her hair hung in ragged brown locks. Her cheeks had a pinched look, and her eyes seemed almost feverish.

"Victor?" Jeremy called, coming down the stairs.

"In the front room," Victor answered without taking his attention off the stranger.

Jeremy came up behind him and asked, "What are you looking at?"

Without moving any closer to the window, Victor pointed out the young woman across the street.

"What about her?" Jeremy inquired. "Is she a nosy neighbor, or some such?"

"No," Victor answered, "I don't know who she is. But she doesn't belong on my street, and she's just been staring over here at the house."

"Perhaps she is mentally deficient," Jeremy suggested.

"I don't think so," Victor said in a low voice, "she feels off."

"May I get a closer look?" Jeremy asked, and without waiting for an answer, he stepped passed Victor, moving closer to the window.

A minute later Jeremy hissed and stepped back.

Victor glanced at the older man, and when he turned back to the woman, he caught sight of her as she slipped around the corner of Alfred's house.

"What was it?" Victor asked, facing Jeremy. "What did you see?"

"She's the one who stole the safe," Jeremy said in a low voice.

Victor didn't respond. Instead, he stepped towards the door.

But Jeremy's hand dropped onto his shoulder, the man's grip strong as he brought Victor to a halt.

"Don't," Jeremy cautioned. "I am afraid it would be a poor decision."

"Why?" Victor demanded, trying to wrench his shoulder away but failing.

"She's not in control of herself," Jeremy answered.

"What?" Victor scoffed. "Who is?"

"Rolf is," Jeremy said, releasing Victor, "and it would be better for you if you don't try and stop her. Not yet."

Victor shook his head, confused. "What do you mean? How can Rolf be in control? He's a ghost!"

"That he is," Jeremy said, limping to the couch and sitting down. "But ghosts can do more than suggest an idea. They can take control if the correct situation presents itself."

Victor hesitated, then walked over and dropped into a wing chair across from the older man.

"You are, I am certain, wondering what such a situation might be," Jeremy said, a sad smile on his face.

Victor nodded.

"There are two occasions when a body might be controlled by a ghost," Jeremy said. "When a mind is feeble, either through some injury or through abuse of say, alcohol, or a narcotic. The other, and far less pleasant, is when there is a fresh corpse. This is far less likely to happen in America, however. It is the hallmark of an Eastern ghost."

"How in God's name do you know that?" Victor asked, unable to keep the horror out of his voice.

The older man sighed, rubbed at his leg and said, "Vietnam."

"What about Vietnam?" Victor asked.

"I tell people that I was injured when I stepped on a mine," Jeremy said, looking past Victor and at the wall. "That is a lie, but it is a believable lie. The truth is far more disturbing, and it would ensure a place in an asylum for me if I made a habit of telling people."

Jeremy paused, and Victor waited for him to continue.

"In 1969," Jeremy said, "I was on patrol. Nothing out of the ordinary. We were sweeping through an area that another unit had already passed through. They had come into contact with a Viet Cong patrol, and there had been several men killed. When we came to the landing zone, there was a small team holding the position, and sitting with the bodies. The wounded had already been taken away, and the team was waiting for a second helicopter to retrieve the dead."

Again Jeremy hesitated, looking down at his leg.

"It turned out that we were near a pagoda, a burial ground for some Vietnamese," the man continued, clearing his throat. "Evidently several of the dead were restless. They took the opportunity to possess the corpses of our dead, and they attacked us. We had the unfortunate luck of coming under attack by a secondary unit of Viet Cong at the same time. We were trapped between the living and the dead. The medevac chopper and its escort of helicopter gunships were the only reason we survived. They chased off the living, and shredded the dead with machine gun fire."

"You're not serious," Victor whispered, but even as the words left his mouth, he knew the statement was foolish, just as he knew Jeremy had spoken the truth.

"I am, unfortunately," Jeremy said with a sigh. "And I can assure you, Victor, that the young woman we saw is not herself. It is Rolf, and he is not yet done with us."

"Why?" Victor asked.

"Because he likes to cause misery," Jeremy replied. "It is as simple and horrific as that."

"But we can't let her get away," Victor said, trying to stifle the sound of desperation in his voice.

"We must," Jeremy said. "We cannot face him. Not yet."

Silence filled the air between them for several minutes, and Victor asked, "How do you know?"

"I have heard of Rolf before," Jeremy answered, "and his story is one of blood and betrayal."

"What did he do?" Victor asked.

"I'll tell you," the older man replied, relaxing into the couch. "But it is not a pleasant tale."

As Jeremy related the history of Rolf, Victor listened and realized the man was right.

Chapter 25: The Story of Rolf

"Rolf Strasse was a sadist," Jeremy said, looking at Victor.

"When he was a young man, only fifteen," Jeremy continued, "the First World War broke out. He was one of the first in Austria to answer the call to arms. Soon he found himself facing off against the Russians and the Italians, and whomever else he was told to fight. It would be a mistake to say he was only proficient in killing. He was an expert at death, and in the art of inflicting pain. There are still photographs of him standing beside men, women, and children he had slaughtered. Some by hanging. Others by shooting. More than a few he set fire to. By the end of the war, he had moved on to knives, enjoying the close and personal nature of the weapon."

"Jesus Christ," Victor whispered.

"I'm certain many people went to their deaths screaming the same," Jeremy said without humor. He cleared his throat and then continued. "No one has been able to ascertain when or how Rolf died. There had been reports of him in Munich, Berlin, Ansbach and other German cities. He moved with the paramilitary organizations, serving as muscle when necessary. More often than not, he was thrilled with work as an interrogator, although his enthusiasm had to be curbed."

Jeremy paused, gathered his thoughts and gave Victor a tight smile. "To give you an idea of the company he kept, Rolf was one of the first adherents to Hitler and his politics. There are some who suspect that Rolf was killed when Hitler purged the Party prior to obtaining the position of Chancellor."

"He was a Nazi," Victor said, and Jeremy saw the younger man shudder.

"Only in the loosest of terms," Jeremy clarified. "If the Weimar Republic would have let him run free with his knives, then he would have been a staunch defender of the republic and fought the Nazis for the sake of the government. No, he was not a Nazi through belief, but merely through opportunity."

"But if he was such a nasty and spiteful maniac," Victor said, sounding confused, "why is he in a child's toy?"

"There are theories about that, of course," Jeremy explained. "First, that the man who executed Rolf had come upon the savage's handiwork during the war, and left the bear there as a sort of tribute to the dead. Another is that he was killed in a toy shop, having sought refuge there when the assassins came for him. And finally, the one I personally believe has the most credence is that he thought it would be more enjoyable. What better way to wreak havoc than from the safety of a child's mechanical toy?"

Jeremy looked at Victor and waited for any questions the man might have. They lapsed into silence, broken finally a few minutes later when Victor asked, "Why is he in that woman's body? Why was he here, watching us?"

"Think about what you have asked," Jeremy said in a gentle voice, "and see if you can answer your own question."

Victor bit down on his lip, his eyes taking on a faraway look.

Jeremy waited, sure the younger man would come to the unfortunate conclusion that was the only answer.

Victor straightened up, his eyes widening.

"He's coming back for me," Victor whispered.

"For us," Jeremy corrected. "He wants us both dead, and the girl has given him a better chance of success in that department."

"What should we do?" Victor asked, glancing at the front door.

"Arm ourselves," Jeremy replied, "and find out who sold Rolf to your wife."

"Why?" Victor asked.

"Because I believe they knew exactly what it was they were selling."

The expression on Victor's face became one of mixed rage and hate, and Jeremy could only hope the man would control himself when they found the seller.

Chapter 26: Home Again

Grant had spent several days at the hotel until he accepted the fact that he had to go home at some point.

The elevator in his building felt smaller than before, a claustrophobic sensation pressed down on him as he waited to reach his floor. When it did, he felt as though he was released from a vice, stumbling out with all of the grace of a dying fish. He put his hand against the wall and then snatched it away.

The wall had been cold. Painfully so.

Mrs. Ducharme came out of her apartment, nodding hello. She was wrapped in a coat, the collar turned up against the chill in the air.

"Terrible in here," she muttered, pausing to speak with him. "There is something wrong with the air conditioning. The super said he is going to investigate it, but who knows when that good for nothing will actually get around to doing it."

"Has it been difficult here?" Grant asked, shivering.

Mrs. Ducharme nodded. "Did you get a new doll?"

He nodded, then realized what she asked and said, "Yes. Why do you ask?"

"I think there may be something wrong with it," Mrs. Ducharme said. "I have heard it each night. It sounds as though she has a recording that malfunctioned. I thought you only collected antique dolls."

"I do," Grant replied. "Someone may have installed a player at some point. I will look into it. Thank you for telling me, Mrs. Ducharme."

She waved the thanks away and said, "You should bundle up tonight, Grant. And drink some soup. This cold is difficult. I would hate for you to come down with something, especially when it is so nice outside."

Grant nodded his agreement, turning his attention to the door of his own apartment. There was no package from Nan East, or anyone else, at his door, and the doorknob was almost too cold to touch when he slid in the key.

The cold air that spilled out of his apartment was brutal, setting his teeth to chatter as he stepped into the apartment. He turned on the light, but nothing happened. Grant flicked the switch up and down several times, wondering if there was a loose connection, but nothing happened.

Dim light filtered in through the shaded windows along the far wall, affording him enough light to go into the kitchen and retrieve his flashlight. He turned it on and used it to guide him down the hallway to Anne's room. The door was closed, and as he stood there great clouds of breath billowed out of his mouth and curled from his nostrils. He tilted his head toward the door, listening.

He heard nothing, and he felt a sense of relief wash over him as the silence greeted him.

Did I overreact? I know I didn't imagine it. Mrs. Ducharme didn't imagine it? Or did she? Did we both? he asked himself. *No. You heard the singing. You spoke with –*

Grant straightened up.

Anne had started to sing. Her words drifted through the door. She was singing once more in French, and the sound was terrifying.

Grant took a cautious step away from the door, and her song ceased.

The doll called out a question in French, but he didn't speak the language, so he couldn't offer up an answer. His breath came in short, shallow gasps as he took another half step down the hall, and Anne spoke again.

The language was still French, but the tone had changed. It was harsh and angry, and as the last syllable reached his ears, the flashlight in his hand died, leaving him in darkness.

Reaching out, Grant found the wall, and he forced himself to turn around. At the far end of the hallway, he saw a dull glow, the last light of the day offering him salvation. He took several steps toward it when he heard the doorknob behind him rattle.

Anne's voice came through the door, a demanding tone to her words as the sentence ended in an unintelligible question.

Grant ran towards the light, his legs leaden and ponderous. Each breath was a challenge and stars exploded around the edges of his vision for want of oxygen. Over his own labored breathing, he heard the door to Anne's room click open.

In spite of the fear gripping him, Grant looked back and wished he hadn't.

The light that promised him safety also glowed in the porcelain cheeks of the doll and burned in her dead eyes. When she saw him, she howled at him in French. Fear wrapped around his heart and squeezed. His body demanded that he stop, that he fight for oxygen and a release from the ghost's grip.

Yet at the same time, Grant knew that if he ceased his attempt at escape, she would kill him. His need to live, his desire to die a natural death and not at the hands of a possessed doll spurred him forward.

Behind him, Grant heard Anne chase after him, the sickening, shuffling sound of a wounded, rabid animal.

Pain erupted in his legs, agony in his knees. It felt as though glass was driven into the soles of his feet with every step, but instead of stopping, Grant pushed himself faster.

He burst out of the hall and into the dining room. The door out was less than twenty feet away, and he ran for it as Anne screamed at him. On the wall over the fireplace, the flat screen television exploded. Vases along the wall shattered, and electricity leaped out of the doorknob as Grant reached for it.

His own shriek of pain and horrified surprise drowned out Anne for a moment, but he fought the instinct to withdraw his hand. Instead, he forced himself to grab it, the stench of burning flesh filling his nose.

Grant wrenched the door open and staggered into the hall, leaving the skin of the palm of his hand fused to the knob. Without hesitation, he reached out, grasped the still hot metal and slammed the door closed.

He collapsed on the carpet and stared at his apartment.

From the other side, he heard the deadbolt click, locking into place. A moment later, he heard Anne as she began to sing again. The song faded as she walked away from the door, his home no longer his, but hers.

Chapter 27: Not Sure of the Situation

"Hey, is that blood on you?" the dealer asked.

"So what?" Sue snapped. "You selling or not?"

The young man shrugged, held out his hand and Sue slapped cash into it.

"Damn, girl," he said, holding up a damp twenty dollar bill, "this one does have blood on it."

"Do you think it's not going to work?" she demanded.

The dealer chuckled. "No, girl, it'll work just fine. You're hardcore. I like that. Name's Danny, you come back if you need some work too."

He handed a small bag of heroin over, and she pocketed it before she responded.

"I don't work on my back," she said.

"No, not you," Danny grinned, flashing a grill of stainless steel on his teeth. "You're too hard. No, you need some real work, some dirty work, you come see me. I'll pay you good. Not just dope either."

"I'll need work," Sue said. "I'll find you."

Danny nodded, and that was the end of their conversation.

She didn't look back as she left Roby Park in Nashua, New Hampshire. Her legs carried her down a thin, narrow street that slipped into the woods and marked the boundary between New Hampshire and Massachusetts. Pepperell was on the other side, and the house she was staying in was there as well.

Sue moved the hand with the heroin in it into the front pocket of her hoodie. She glanced down at the sweatshirt, not sure where the blood on it had originated from.

I'll ask Rolf when I get back, Sue thought. She had been blacking out during her nods, not remembering anything for a long time after she shot up.

Rolf always knew what she had done.

She smiled, nodding to herself. The bear always made sure she was okay. He took care of her.

Sue relaxed a little, but she quickened her pace. She was eager to be back, safe and tucked away.

Less than half an hour later, she stepped out of the woods and into the back yard of the house. It was a white colonial, left empty by a family off on some vacation. She and Rolf had been lucky to find it. The place had been packed full of new electronics, too, and she had moved it all. It was easier to fence stolen goods when no one reported them gone.

Grinning, Sue jogged up the back steps, nudged open the door and hurried inside.

Rolf was on the island of the kitchen, exactly where she had left him.

"Hey," she said, dropping down onto a stool.

"Hello," the bear said, chuckling, "did you get your medicine?"

"I did," Sue answered, taking the heroin out and dropping it onto the island. Her kit, the needle, spoon, and lighter plus the rubber tubing she used to get high were there. An itch blossomed in the crook of her arm as she looked at it.

"There is no need to stand on ceremony," Rolf purred. "You should take your medicine."

She nodded and took off her sweatshirt, then remembered the blood.

"Hey, do you know why there's blood all over this?" she asked, tying the tubing around her upper arm.

"A bloody nose, I am afraid," Rolf said sadly, "it did not stop for a long time."

"I bet," Sue said. It was a drawback of being a junkie. One of many. Without any further questions, she began to fix her medicine.

***

Rolf found it interesting to be in control of the young woman's body. It responded sluggishly at first, as always, and he knew part of it was the amount of heroin she injected. Her doses, he had noticed, were always increased.

But she was malleable, and it entertained him to watch her destroy herself. In addition to that, she also provided a body for his own use.

With Sue well within the grasp of heroin, Rolf stood up and moved forward several spaces, her legs moving slowly. A moment later and he reached the counter top. He eyed the butcher's block appreciatively for a moment, then chose a skinning knife. With the cutlery in hand, Rolf walked out of the kitchen and descended the basement stairs.

Mr. Gregory Burke was naked and bound to a chair. Over the past four days, Mr. Burke had watched Rolf butcher his wife and three children, as well as the family dog and cat. Mr. Burke had not wanted to watch, of course, but Rolf had removed the man's eyelids and kept the eyes themselves well lubricated.

When Mr. Burke saw Rolf in the form of Sue, he let out a moan. He couldn't scream because Rolf had removed the man's tongue the day before, and then devoured it raw in front of him. Rolf had savored every bite, the girl's taste buds a pure delight after having been deprived of his own for so long.

The terror in Mr. Burke's eyes was pure as Rolf sat down in front of him. Rolf smiled and held up the skinning knife. Mr. Burke winced as much as his bonds would allow him.

"Tell me, Mr. Burke," Rolf said, "do you think I will be able to skin you all in one go, or perhaps have to do it in sections?"

Mr. Burke moaned again, shaking his head violently.

"You're right, talking about it won't give us an answer," Rolf said, standing up. "Let's find out, shall we?"

The answer was sections.

Chapter 28: Commack, Long Island, New York

Stefan stood in the middle of the house and listened.

He heard nothing, and he nodded with satisfaction.

The dead were still, which was what he needed them to be. He had made them a promise, that there would soon be someone there to prey upon. Whether it was true or not didn't matter. It kept them quiet.

Stefan knew that the Louisiana buyer would show up in person to return Anne, as well as the teapot. It was the only way for the buyer to be certain that she wouldn't hunt him down again afterwards. There was always the chance that Anne would have finished the man off before that, but Stefan doubted he would be so lucky. The next best-case scenario would be the man traveling to Commack without the doll. In that situation, the dead in the house would finish him off, and Anne would be set loose on some unsuspecting person in Louisiana.

Stefan smiled at the thought and went about the house, double-checking the traps he had laid. There were two in each room, a guarantee that the buyer would trigger at least one of them. And they were innocuous, subtle, not a single one of them spoke of the dangers that lay within.

The walking stick propped in the corner by the front door, the Jaeger pipe on the table beside the stick. A cup and matching saucer from the coronation of Elizabeth the Second. On a table in the den was a remote control. Beside that lay a copy of National Geographic from 1962. The cherub lamp in the den and the tin soldiers in the kitchen.

Minor ghosts. Individually, they were nothing.

Combined, they were deadly.

As soon as the man was in the house one of them was sure to be triggered. And it wouldn't take much, nothing more than a careless pants' leg brushing the stick. A hand bumping against the pipe.

Stefan removed one last item from his bag. An old and well-used coffee mug, a large letter 'E' stenciled on it. This had been the last item his father had ordered, and it had arrived shortly after his death. Stefan's mother had kept it with her, never having the heart to place it in the room with Ivan Denisovich's other ghosts.

Stefan set the mug down in the kitchen, nodded to himself and retreated to the front door.

"Be patient," Stefan told the dead and left the house. He closed the front door and pinned a note to it. Stefan left the porch, walked halfway down the front walk and turned around. He examined the building, searching for flaws, anything that might make the buyer hesitate.

The house looked as any house in a middle-class neighborhood should. While the home was older, having been built in the first part of the twentieth century, it was well-kept. The grass was cut, the siding recently painted a soft blue. White shutters hung on either side of the windows, and there was a welcome sign on the front lawn beside a statue of a frog lounging in the sun.

Every aspect the property screamed middle America, and it brought a smile to Stefan's face. He turned away and went to the car. It was a rental, borrowed under a false name and paid with cash, as well as a large bribe. The previous vehicle, the one stolen for the sole purpose of eliminating Collier, had been abandoned on the Massachusetts and New York border.

Stefan's thoughts went back to the rental and he doubted he could trust the woman who had rented him the car to remain quiet – should he be investigated at some point – so he would murder her when he returned home.

The idea of strangling her made him smile, and he whistled as he climbed into the car.

For the first time in several days, he was feeling happy again.

Chapter 29: Darkness in the Street

At midnight, Victor left the house.

He despised being inside the structure, and he found it difficult to be there even when he had Jeremy for company. Erin was still everywhere he looked, in every smell, in the touch of the sheets against his skin.

Victor put his hands in his pockets and walked down the street. A few lights were on in his neighbor's houses, but he was the only one out. Several cats trotted past him, moving in and out of the shadows and pointedly ignoring him. It took him a moment to comprehend that they all had their tails down, ears pressed flat to their heads.

And they ran from the right side of the street to the left.

They're afraid, Victor paused, slowing down and taking his hands out of his pockets. He glanced over at the opposite side of the street, trying to see what was frightening the animals.

At first, he saw nothing out of the ordinary.

Then a dog barked, a harsh sound full of anger and fear. A chain rattled and the canine's complaints rose to a frenzied pitch.

Within seconds, a person walked out of the shadows of the closest house, glancing back the way they had come.

It was a young woman.

The same individual Victor had seen several days before. A young woman, Jeremy believed, who was playing host to the spirit of Rolf.

As she stepped into the light, the young woman turned around and looked at Victor. She stopped, smiled and said in a low voice, "Why hello, Victor. Such a pleasure to see you. I thought I was going to have to break into your house to have a conversation with you."

Victor eyed the woman, who was thin and sickly, but her eyes burned brightly with a fierce energy that made him uncomfortable. He wanted to run, but the expression on her face made him doubt he would make it back safely to his house.

"You should be kind to me," Rolf said, chuckling. "I can make your death either fast or slow, or some unhappy medium. You could let me know. I am quite open to requests."

Victor never took his eyes off the young woman, who continued to approach him. Her steps were short, her attention always fixed on him.

"Do you like this vessel?" Rolf asked lasciviously. "Is she not equal, no, does she not surpass your dead wife?"

Victor bit back a reply, refusing to be baited into a conversation with the ghost.

"Why do you not speak with me?" Rolf asked, a playful tone in his voice. "Are you afraid of me? Afraid of this thin woman? You should be. I'm going to kill you soon."

The cold surety with which the statement was made threatened Victor's composure, but he managed to retain it. Anger flared up as he remembered this was the being who had slain his wife and who, if Jeremy's information had been correct, had been a butcher when alive as well.

"You think so?" Victor snarled, clenching his hands into fists. "You think you're going to kill me? I don't care how strong your little junkie is, but if you come near me, I will beat you to death."

Rolf's eyes widened in surprise, a smirk of appreciation appearing on the girl's face.

"I appreciate such sentiments," Rolf said, "I believe those were the same uttered before I was assassinated. Though there was a squad of soldiers who came for me."

Rolf looked to the left and then to the right with exaggerated turns of the girl's head.

"Ah," Rolf said in mock sadness, "it looks like you're alone, without even the shade of your wife to keep you company."

Victor stepped forward, and Rolf laughed, a look of eager anticipation spreading. Then the expression faltered, and in the light of the street lamp, the girl's eyes changed. The irises flickered, and what had once been a stunning green, shifted into a pale blue then back to green.

"No!" Rolf hissed, his head jerking from side to side. "She can't come out of it! Not yet!"

The girl tried to stumble away, fell to a knee, got back up, twisted around and let out an angry howl. "No!"

Her eyes changed again to the pale blue, and stayed that way.

The girl straightened up and in a frightened voice asked, "What's going on? Where am I?"

"You're in Pepperell," Victor said, not sure what he should do. "Do you know what day it is?"

She shook her head. "No. I'm not sure what day it is, or what I'm doing here. How did I get here? Who the hell are you?"

The girl took a step back, glancing around her. "I just want to go back. Okay? I just want Rolf. He's taking care of me."

"The bear is?" Victor asked softly.

"Yes," she said, head bobbing up and down. Then she looked at him, shocked. "Wait. How did you know he was a bear?"

Victor hesitated, unsure if he should tell her all of it, or only part, or if it would even matter. Any of it.

"I know," Victor said, struggling to get the words out, "because he killed my wife."

The girl shook her head, glanced down at her blood-stained sweat-shirt and looked up at Victor with an expression of pure horror on her face. "This isn't my blood, is it?"

"I don't know," Victor said. "What's your name?"

"What?" she snapped, her voice rising in panic.

"Your name," Victor said in a soft, soothing tone. "Tell me your name."

"Sue," she whispered, looking around.

"Sue, I'm Victor," he said, "why don't we go to my house, okay?"

"Why?" There was no sign of trust in her eyes.

"You look like you need to eat," Victor said, "and I think a friend of mine can help you."

She seemed to shrink within herself, shuddering. "I need a fix. That's what I need."

"Do you have any on you?" Victor asked.

Sue straightened up, caught off guard by the question. She patted her front pocket, and her shoulders relaxed. "Yeah, but I don't have my kit."

"My wife," Victor said, speaking slowly, "she was a diabetic. I haven't gotten rid of any of her stuff."

"You'd let me shoot up?" Sue asked, confused. "Why?"

"I need to know about Rolf," Victor answered, "and I need you to talk to my friend about it. If that means you go into the upstairs bathroom and shoot up, then that's what happens."

Sue scratched at her arm, then nodded. "Yeah. Sure, let's do it."

"This way," Victor said, and he led her towards his house.

Chapter 30: The Teapot Arrives

Grant went to the post office and had his mail forwarded to his office. He was unsure what to do about Anne since she had taken over his home, and he needed the teapot to find the seller.

Grant moved his hand the wrong way and bit back a scream. His right hand was bandaged, but the pain was significant. He resisted the urge to get out the Ativan they had prescribed. It clouded his thoughts and made it difficult for him to work. He couldn't afford to be dim-witted when the teapot arrived.

A knock on the door interrupted his thoughts and forced him to call out, "Come in."

The UPS delivery man entered the office nodding hello and placing a package down on the desk top.

Once the door closed, Grant dragged the package closer, afraid that it was nothing more than antique hardware or some other such necessity for a project. But it wasn't, it was the teapot.

And it had a return address for Commack, Long Island in New York.

After several awkward attempts, he managed to open the box, and he removed the teapot. It was exactly as it had been described, and he had a sudden revulsion for the item.

He wasn't sure what to do with it, if he should bring it to the address and leave it in front of the door. Grant wasn't sure what would happen, or what the ghost that resided within it might do.

What if it only makes the ghost mad? Grant thought, horrified.

Then an idea came to him, and he sighed with relief.

He replaced the teapot in its package, then gathered it up and left the office. When he reached the main lobby of his building, Grant asked the doorman to call for a cab. The box grew colder in his arms as he held it, and fear began to build in him. There was a sensation that the ghost in the teacup had realized it was somewhere new, that it wanted to be out.

Grant didn't want that, not in the least. He needed it to remain silent and docile until he could get assistance.

He paced the length of the lobby until the cab arrived, and when it did, he hurried out to the vehicle, clambering into the back as best as his injury would allow. When the cabbie asked Grant for the destination, he gave the man Leanne Le Monde's address.

She was the only one he knew who could help him with the teapot before the situation became dire.

The ride to her house in the French Quarter took far longer than it had the first time when he had driven himself. Or that's what his mind told him as the cab cruised along the narrow streets, stopping and starting again for the pedestrians which crowded the pavement.

When he reached her house, and the cabbie had let him out, Grant hurried up to her front door, ringing the old brass bell that hung to the left. Several minutes passed, and Grant rang the bell again.

His heart beat increased as seconds passed again to minutes. The palm of his left hand became slick with sweat as fear that she was out crept into his thoughts.

Just as the thought entered his mind, the door opened.

Leanne Le Monde looked down at him, saw the package in his arms and the bandage on his hand, and shook her head.

"Your situation is worse, is it not?" she asked, an imperious tone to her words.

Grant could only nod.

"What do you need from me, young man?" she asked. "Did I not tell you to dispose of the doll?"

"I couldn't," Grant said, his voice hoarse as he showed her his hand. "I was lucky to escape the apartment. She wanted to kill me."

"You use the wrong tense," she corrected, "Anne still wants to kill you, and she will do so as soon as you afford her the opportunity."

"Please," Grant begged, "how do I get rid of her?"

"You need to speak to a professional in this type of situation," she replied, "and that is not me."

Leanne began to close the door, and Grant said, "Wait! Won't you let me in?"

She nodded toward the package. "I'll let nothing like that cross my threshold, young man. I have not lived so long by taking such foolish chances."

"Who can I talk to?" Grant implored. "Who can help me get rid of her?"

The old woman's hard façade cracked, and in a soft voice, she said, "Look up a man named Jeremy Rhinehart. He knows how to take care of problems such as yours. I do not know how much he costs, but I assume it is a large amount. And you would do wise to mention that I recommended him, else he might charge even more."

Before Grant could ask her anymore questions, Leanne Le Monde closed the door, the tumbling click of the deadbolt loud even against the back drop of the French Quarter.

Chapter 31: Learning about the Bear

Victor felt unwell. His head throbbed and his throat was sore, there was a dryness in his mouth, and his tongue felt larger than normal.

In the guestroom on the second floor, where Jeremy had so recently stayed, the heroin addict lay on the bed. Sue was, as she had said to him before she shot up, on the nod. It was an unattractive sight to see. Mucus ran unchecked from her nose, her mouth was open with spittle leaking out one corner, and her eyes were rolled up, revealing the whites to any who bothered to look closely.

From what he had read online, Victor knew she would be sick when she woke up. Violently so. He had brought her a bucket to throw up in when she awakened, but he had a fear she would aspirate while on her high.

He had gone up several times to check on her, turning her head once to make certain she didn't die.

Victor had left the hall light on so she would be able to see when she woke up, without the glare of the bed lamp in her eyes. He waited for her to descend the stairs, or for Jeremy to knock on the front door.

There was a fear that the next person who knocked wouldn't be Jeremy. That it would be some stranger with brilliant green eyes, possessed by the malignant spirit of Rolf. The dead man had no love for Victor, and it seemed as though he was intent on murder.

The fact that there was no way he could protect himself from an attack left Victor with a sharp, biting sense of paranoia. He had enough food to last for several days, but eventually he would have to leave the house, and the thought terrified him.

A sharp knock on the door caused him to leap off the couch.

He looked at the door, wondering if he should answer it.

Again, a knock sounded a hard, authoritative rap that made Victor's decision for him.

He walked to the door, took a deep, steadying breath, and opened it.

A uniformed police officer stood there, her radio squawking with unintelligible chatter. She had blonde hair pulled back into a tight bun and a body camera that was aimed at Victor. Her sharp features were set into a serious visage and her hazel eyes were focused on Victor.

"Good evening," she said, "my name is Officer Lee of the Pepperell Police Department, and you are being recorded on my body camera. We're going through the neighborhood searching for this woman."

As Officer Lee lifted up a piece of paper with an image of a much healthier Sue Jeffries on it, Victor saw that there were other officers canvassing the street.

"Yes," Victor said, nodding, "I saw her earlier. I offered her something to eat and the use of my phone. She looked like she could use both."

Officer Lee put the picture away and asked, "May I come in?"

"Sure," Victor said, stepping aside and leaving the door open.

Lee's eyes darted around the main room, saw only evidence of Victor's habitation, and came back to his face as she drew out a notepad and pen. She flipped it open, took his name, phone number, and birthdate, and asked him for specifics about his interaction with Sue. Victor left out any information about Rolf and the offer to inject herself in his house and fabricated a story about her eating a small meal of left-overs and using his phone.

"Do you know who she called?" Lee asked.

Victor shook his head. "She took the phone in the other room, spoke to someone for about a minute, then came back in and handed it to me. I asked if she needed a cab or a ride, but she said she was fine. She had spoken with a friend, she told me, and that this friend would pick her up down by town hall."

Lee nodded, wrote the information down and then she hesitated and asked, "How are you holding up?"

The question caught him off guard, and he stuttered as he asked, "What do you mean?"

Lee gave him a small smile. "I was one of the responding officers to your wife, Mr. Daniels."

"Oh," he whispered. His throat clicked audibly when he swallowed before he answered, "I'm not holding up that well, actually, Officer. But thank you, thank you for asking."

"Sure thing, Mr. Daniels," she said, putting her pen and notepad away. "And thank you for the information."

A sense of guilt flashed through him as he nodded. "Anytime. Let me know if I can be of any more help."

Officer Lee smiled and left his house.

Victor closed and locked the door behind her. He wandered back to the couch, dropped down into it, and hoped Jeremy arrived sooner rather than later. Having Sue in the house was no longer just a burden, but detrimental as well. Victor had no intention of being charged with obstruction or harboring a fugitive, or whatever other charge he might fall under with having Sue upstairs.

He needed Jeremy to get to the house, find out what Sue remembered about her interactions with Rolf, and then drop her off in Boston, Massachusetts or Manchester, New Hampshire. Somewhere far away from Pepperell.

A lighter knock sounded on the front door. It was a familiar tone, and Victor sighed, knowing it was Jeremy on the other side.

Victor hastened to the door, opened it, and was relieved to see the older man. Jeremy leaned on his cane, stepped inside and closed the door behind him.

"Why are there police all over your neighborhood?" Jeremy asked.

"Because of the girl," Victor answered, motioning toward the stairs.

Jeremy looked surprised and then asked, "Is she awake?"

"Not yet," Victor said, but then the sound of Sue vomiting filled the house.

"Ah," Jeremy said, "the familiar noises of heroin addiction. Come, Victor, let us prepare some tea. She'll need something hot and soothing in her when she's done."

Victor looked at him, surprised.

Jeremy gave him a tight smile, patted his bad leg and said, "Opioid addiction is a difficult burden. It took me years to wean myself off the morphine they had prescribed to me for my injury. I am well-familiar with side-effects of opiates. Now, let's make that tea."

Victor could only nod, and follow Jeremy into the kitchen.

Chapter 32: A Conversation with a Junkie

Jeremy sat in a chair in the spare bedroom. The only light came from the hallway, and it barely revealed the features of the young woman on the bed in front of him. She had accepted the tea in silence, as did he.

"Who are you?" she asked, her voice raw and pained.

"Jeremy," he replied.

"You're the one he wanted me to talk to," she said.

"I am," Jeremy agreed.

"So," she said, her voice bitter, "what do you want to talk about?"

"The bear," Jeremy said, sipping his tea, "I'd like to talk to you about Rolf."

Even in the dim light, he was able to see her shudder, and he wondered how much she remembered. Or how much she suspected.

"I don't know too much," she said after a minute. "He was good. You know? He said the right things to me, told me it was alright to take my medicine. I think he was using me, though. When I was high."

"Yes," Jeremy agreed, "I am quite certain he was. He needs an incapacitated mind to take control of a body. When you're on the nod, he can move right in. It's like borrowing someone's car, but in your case, it was your body."

"Oh my God," she whispered. "What if he had me doing bad things? I mean, my sweatshirt is covered in blood."

Jeremy sighed. "Then I would have to say he did indeed have you do as you feared."

"My body," she said, looking down at herself. "Oh no, that means he used my hands. My fingerprints are going to be everywhere. No one will believe I didn't do it!"

Panic flooded her voice, and the teacup tumbled out of her hands.

"Sue," Jeremy said, "you need to calm down."

"All the evidence is going to point at me!" she shrieked.

Victor's footsteps sounded on the stairs and in a moment, he was in the doorway, blocking what little light there was.

"Sue," Jeremy said, "I need you to lower your voice. The police may still be in the neighborhood, and if they hear you screaming, they're going to come back."

The young woman sobbed, but no longer screamed. Victor stepped into the room and off to the side, allowing the hall light back in. For several minutes, Sue continued to cry on the bed, and then she was done.

She sniffled, straightened up and wiped her nose with the back of her hand. After a long, shuddering breath, Sue asked, "What now?"

"What do you mean?" Victor asked.

Sue turned her attention to him.

"I mean," she said without any sort of intonation, "that I need to know what's going to happen to me. Do I run or go to the police? Do I go and commit suicide, or maybe get one last bag and give myself an overdose? From what I can see, I'm pretty much done here. Cops will have a field day with me, especially when I tell them I was possessed by a ghost."

She let out a short, sharp bark of a laugh.

Jeremy eyed her warily for the sound had been tainted with madness.

"I need you to listen to me," Jeremy said, her eyes moving from Victor to lock onto him. "Can you do that?"

She nodded.

"Excellent," Jeremy said, "what I need you to do is to tell me everything, everything you can possibly remember about your time with Rolf. What you spoke of and what you did, every part of it."

Sue snorted, shaking her head. "That's just it. I can't remember, not a damned thing. I could have done anything or nothing. He told me I had a nose bleed, which is why there was so much blood on my sweatshirt. But it must have been someone else's."

"Sue," Jeremy started.

"No," she snapped, cutting him off. "I want out of here, as soon as possible. Can you do that? Can you at least get me into Lowell so I can catch the train into Boston?"

"Yes," Jeremy said, "but will you please at least try to remember?"

Sue leaned forward on the bed, snarling, "I can't remember anything. Nothing. Not a thing. Now either get me to Lowell or let me out of the damned house so I can get there. I can't waste any more time."

Jeremy sighed, used his cane to help him get to his feet, and nodded. "Very well. Give us a few minutes, please. We'll see what we can do about a ride for you."

He left the bedroom and Victor followed. They walked down to the first floor in silence, each of them taking a seat in the living room.

"Do you think she's telling the truth?" Victor asked.

"Mm? Oh, yes, I certainly do," Jeremy said, rubbing absently at his hip. "The problem is what she will do with herself. I'm worried she may attempt suicide, and I do not want that on my conscience. Then again, we don't have the right to keep her here against her will, and I think that calling for medical help may be akin to shooting ourselves in the foot. She would certainly use the assistance you gave her as a threat if she felt it necessary."

"Is there something you suggest then?" Victor asked a note of frustration in his voice.

"I will give her a ride into Lowell," Jeremy said, "although I will try and see if she can at least wait until the morning. It would be better for her to be cleaned up and mingling with the rest of the morning commuters on the train into Boston. Such an attempt to elude the police would be unsuspected by them, and might actually allow her to get away."

"What do you think he had her do?" Victor asked, glancing back at the stairs.

"Knowing what he has done in the past," Jeremy said, "I would rather not hazard a guess. I have enough nightmares of my own without imagining anymore."

"Well," Victor said, sighing, "let's hope we can get her away from here without any trouble."

"My hope as well," Jeremy replied. He looked at the stairs, then to the front door, and he prayed that Rolf was still trapped within the bear.

Chapter 33: Slipping Away

The window to the spare bedroom opened out onto the roof of a side porch. Sue was thrilled when the sash went up without a sound, and at the ease with which she was able to remove the screen. She set the aluminum frame onto the bed and went silently back to the window. Her body was still recovering from her last high, but the food she had gotten in her before that, as well as the meals she had eaten with Rolf, had given her a surprising amount of energy.

Sue slipped out the window, lowered herself down onto the roof and paused there, hands keeping her steady on the asphalt shingles. She listened for noise from within the house that would have told her the two men had heard her, and she scanned the street for any sign of lingering police.

Sue didn't see any law enforcement, and the house was silent.

She slipped forward along the roof, saw that the windows below her were dark, and eased herself over the edge. For a moment she hung there by her fingers, then let go, dropping the last few feet to the ground, the tall grass deadening the sound of her landing.

She stayed in the shadow of Victor's home, his neighbor's house dark as she hurried along towards his back yard. When she reached the corner of the house, she hesitated, took a deep breath, and then sprinted towards the hedges that marked the end of Victor's property. Her body was tense as she ran, ready for the audible click of a motion sensor light coming on.

Yet neither Victor nor his neighbor seemed to have one, and she made it to the hedge without being noticed.

She covered her mouth as she took in great gulps of air. After several minutes, she pushed her way through the thick bushes and into an open field. She found herself looking at a baseball diamond, the backstop illuminated by the moon. A pair of dugouts, painted deep green, flanked the baselines, and beyond that was a parking lot.

There were no cars or people to be seen, and Sue let out a sigh of relief. She kept to the bushes, following the curve of the outfield toward the chain-link fence that marked the boundaries of the field. Briefly, she contemplated climbing the fence, but she saw an open gate behind the first base dugout, and she hurried to it.

Sue had reached first base when she heard a noise in the closest dugout. She froze, hoping it was an animal.

"Hello, Sue," a man said, his voice a high, nasal pitch.

He came up out of the dugout, a short, squat man who looked as though he had been chiseled out of brick, with far too much left over on his stomach. In his left hand, he held an aluminum baseball bat. He wore a pair of dark blue slacks, and a lighter blue shirt with a nametag and company patch on it that she couldn't quite make out in the moonlight.

"How have you been?" he asked, stepping between her and the exit.

"Who the hell are you?" she snapped.

He grinned. "It's Rolf, Sue. Rolf. Although I am sure, I sound different. This man's voice is nothing like my own. But, as you know, the old saying is true. Beggars can't be choosers. He's not nearly as lithe or nimble as you. But he does get the job done. A strong brute. And he likes his wine. *In vino veritas*, correct?"

Sue shook her head, confused and afraid.

"I want to go," she told the dead man. "I just want to leave. I'm trying to get away."

"What did you tell them about me, Sue?" Rolf asked, stepping closer.

Sue moved back, heart pounding with a growing fear.

"What did you say about our time together?" he whispered. "Hm?"

She stuttered as she answered, "Nothing. I swear. I didn't tell them anything about you."

His nostrils flared, and he chuckled.

"I smell a lie," Rolf said in a gentle voice. "A pungent and foul falsehood. Wouldn't you agree, young Sue?"

She shook her head violently, her eyes flickering from left to right as she sought a means of escape.

"Look at me, girl," he said, his voice soft and sweet, "turn your eyes back to Rolf now."

Hyperventilating, Sue did so, and she saw a gentle smile on Rolf's face as he swung the bat in long, lazy arcs from right to left and back again.

"Would I hurt you?" he asked, his voice soothing. "Would I do anything to you, my dear, little friend?"

Sue didn't answer, fear freezing her in place.

His lips curled into a smile, and he whispered, "Of course I would."

And before Sue could move, Rolf leaped forward, the bat crashing down upon her head. As she collapsed to the grass, the world suddenly black, Sue heard the sound of the bat racing through the air, and then there was nothing more for her to be afraid of.

Chapter 34: A Phone Call from NOLA

The sound of sirens had interrupted the conversation between Jeremy and Victor. Loud and piercing, the noise of the emergency vehicles told Victor that the incident was close and a sudden worry overtook him.

He stood up from the couch and Jeremy looked at him, asking, "What's wrong?"

"I want to make sure Sue's still here," Victor answered, and he hurried up the stairs.

Even without turning on the light he knew she was gone. The overhead lamp merely confirmed the fact, showing him the details. On the rumpled sheets of the bed lay the screen of the window. The window was open, the cool night air flowing in without impediment.

His shoulders sagged as he switched off the light and returned to the couch. Jeremy looked at him and said, "She's gone."

Victor nodded. "Probably right after we left the room."

Jeremy frowned and said, "Those sirens are for her."

"That would be my guess," Victor said, shaking his head. He felt uncomfortable as he asked, "Do you think it was Rolf?"

"It is what I would assume," Jeremy said, rubbing at his hip. "I can only hope that it was quick."

Victor shuddered at the idea of the young woman's murder, yet another life taken by the beast bound to the bear.

Jeremy's cellphone rang, and the man drew it out of his pocket. Victor watched as the man frowned at the number on the screen and then answered the call anyway. Not wanting to intrude on the conversation, Victor stood up and left the room for the kitchen. In spite of it being well past midnight, he started a pot of coffee, knowing that he wouldn't sleep, at least not without the aid of some sort of drug.

And he had no desire to take anything.

At least not yet.

The coffee was ready before Jeremy finished his call, the man's voice rising and falling. Several times there were long lulls in the conversation, but they always ended.

Finally, after twenty minutes, Jeremy came into the kitchen. He raised an eyebrow at the coffee, hesitated, then got himself a cup. When he sat down at the table across from Victor, he said, "We may have gotten a little break concerning who sold Rolf to your wife."

Victor's hands shook, and he put the cup down on the table before he spilled any of the coffee. "What do you mean?"

"I was just on the phone with a man named Grant, from New Orleans," Jeremy explained. "He told me that an old friend and colleague of mine referred me to him. Evidently, he recently purchased a haunted doll from an unknown seller. The doll tried to kill him."

"Good God," Victor whispered.

Jeremy nodded. "What he wanted from me was the removal of the doll from his apartment. It turns out he is unable to go home. I persuaded him to tell me more about the purchase, and when he told me about it, and the fact that he bought another item from the same seller in hopes that he might return both, I thought we might be fortunate."

"How so?" Victor asked.

"Grant explained that he managed to get a return address for the seller," Jeremy said. "It is an address in Commack, Long Island. He is hopeful of returning both items to the seller. I told him I would be happy to go to New Orleans to assist him with his haunted doll, but only if he allowed me to accompany him to Long Island. He was more than happy to agree."

"May I come along?" Victor asked, trying to keep the desperation out of his voice.

Jeremy smiled. "I was hoping you would. Not only for the company but for the fact that I dislike the idea of you being here whilst Rolf is on the loose. I can only surmise that he will make a concerted effort to kill you, especially now that Sue is probably dead."

Victor nodded. "When would we leave?"

"It would be a matter of me canceling appointments for the next week or so, and booking the flights," Jeremy said, "and whatever you might need to do in regards to work."

"I can work on the way, when we're there, and on the way to Long Island," Victor stated. "I'm ready to go whenever you are."

"Well then, my new traveling companion," Jeremy said, raising his cup in salute, "let us prepare for our adventure."

Victor nodded and finished his coffee.

His hands, he noticed, were no longer shaking.

Chapter 35: The Arrival of Assistance

Grant stood in the terminal of the Louis Armstrong Airport, waiting for the arrival of a man he hoped would help rid him of the scourge of Anne. He held a sign in his hands with the names Jeremy Rhinehart and Victor Daniels on it, and felt ridiculous. Grant thought it could have been worse if he looked as foolish as half the people he saw; phones pressed to their ears while they scanned the crowd for friends and family.

He reminded himself that he shouldn't complain. Jeremy had agreed to come down to Louisiana immediately, and his only request was to meet the seller.

"Grant?"

Called back to reality by the sound of his name, Grant looked up and saw a man in his sixties or seventies walking toward him with the assistance of a cane. A much younger man, who looked as though he hadn't slept for weeks, kept pace with him.

"That's me," Grant said, lowering the sign with silent thanks. He dropped it into a nearby trashcan and then extended his hand. Both Jeremy and Victor shook it in turn. "Thank you for coming."

"I've always enjoyed New Orleans," Jeremy said, his words spoken with the precise, nasal intonation of a native New Englander. "Are we far from your home?"

Grant shook his head as he said, "No. Not at all. But don't you need to rest, or do some research?"

"Not at all," Jeremy said with a tight smile. "All we need is a trip to the French Quarter. There are certain shops in the Quarter where I will be able to procure what I need for your doll."

"I'll be right back," Victor said, speaking for the first time. "I need the restroom."

After the man had left, Grant turned to Jeremy and asked, "Is he alright?"

Jeremy shook his head. "The same individual who sold you Anne sold Victor's wife a possessed toy. It convinced her to kill herself."

"God in Heaven," Grant said, glancing back at the way Victor had gone. "When was this?"

"Only a short time ago," Jeremy said. "He is a remarkably resilient man. I believe he will be of great assistance to me. Especially with the taking of Anne."

"I certainly hope so," Grant said. "She is quite brutal."

"The fact that she let you live for so long without an attempt on your life is impressive," Jeremy stated, "and it is not a fact which should be overlooked. She found you appealing, Grant. Ah, here is my young friend now."

Victor had returned, his face damp and his hair slicked back.

"I get over a flight quicker if I wash my face as soon as I land," Victor explained, his face reddening a shade.

"I find a good glass of bourbon does that for me," Grant said. The three of them chuckled together at the statement and Grant led them along the hallway towards the exit. Victor flagged down a cab, and they got into the back.

"Where to?" the cabbie asked.

"630 Royal Street, please," Jeremy said.

The cabbie pulled away from the curb, and Grant looked at Jeremy.

"That's M.S. Rau Antiques," he said after a moment.

"It is indeed," Jeremy said, nodding.

"What are you going to find there that will help you with what you need?" Grant asked, confused. "I shop from them when I'm designing. They don't strike me as the type to carry ghost hunting items."

Jeremy glanced at him, a small smile playing on his face. "Grant, when you want something of quality, you go to the best. Simply because the piece wasn't made for ghost hunting does not mean that it cannot be. John Ruskin stated that you get what you pay for. I intend to buy the best, so therefore it makes sense to shop at only the best. Wouldn't you agree?"

"Yes," Grant said, scratching the back of his head with his good hand, "I'm just confused."

"You need to relax," Jeremy said. "So long as I am not confused, everything is going to be fine."

"And if you get confused?" Victor asked.

"Then we all need to run," Jeremy said.

A man wearing shorts and painted to look like a skeleton danced by the cab, shaking a long staff topped with a skull on it at the vehicle.

Jeremy clapped his hands and let out a chuckle. "My God, I've missed New Orleans."

"Do you like it here?" Grant asked.

Jeremy nodded.

"Do you visit the city often?" Grant asked, settling back into the sprung seat of the cab.

"No," Jeremy admitted, "not for almost twenty years."

"How come?" Victor asked, turning his head away from the window.

"Hm?" Jeremy said.

"Why don't you visit more often?" Grant said, picking up the thread of the question.

"Ah, a silly reason," Jeremy said, turning his attention back to the world outside of the cab.

Grant smiled. "And what sort of silly reason might that be?"

"I spoke with a voodoo priest in the French Quarter back in 1975," Jeremy said.

Grant rolled his eyes. He hated people who dragged out an answer to what should have been an obvious line of questioning.

"Did the priest say something?" Grant asked. "Prophesize some sort of event?"

"He did indeed," Jeremy replied.

"Good God, Jeremy," Victor said, sighing, "can't you just tell him what he wants to know?"

Jeremy turned in his seat and gave Grant a wry smile. "Is there something you wish to know, Grant?"

Trying not to let his frustration be heard, he answered, "Yes. What was it that the voodoo priest told you in 1975 that has kept you from visiting here?"

"Ah," Jeremy said. "There we have it. A nice, pointed, direct question. To which I shall give a nice, pointed, direct answer."

Grant waited for Jeremy to continue, and when he realized that Jeremy was teasing him, he bit his tongue to keep from saying something sharp.

After a moment, Jeremy chuckled, looked back out the window, and said, "The priest told me that I would die in New Orleans, Grant. And he said that it wouldn't be pleasant. Not in the least."

The cabbie turned on a sports radio station, and the men rode the rest of the way to the French Quarter in silence.

Chapter 36: On Royal Street

Victor stood outside of the antique store and waited while Jeremy and the new man, Grant, shopped. Jeremy had said nothing else about the warning passed on by the voodoo priest, years earlier, and he had remained tight-lipped about what exactly he had hoped to find in the store. Grant, who was familiar with the current management, had accompanied him.

Victor struggled with a growing sense of irritation.

Rolf was still in Massachusetts, and they were on the Mississippi looking for an object to help Jeremy with a haunted doll.

And Victor wanted to help the man, but more than that, he wanted to stop Rolf and find a way to destroy the ghost, or at least imprison him forever.

"You are thinking of Rolf," Jeremy said, speaking slightly behind Victor and causing him to jump in surprise.

"Damn," Victor said, his heart thundering against his chest. "You scared the hell out of me."

Jeremy smiled an apology and Victor looked past him at Grant. The other man carried a large package in his arms, the item wrapped in heavy brown paper. There was a curious expression of confusion, admiration, and trepidation on the man's face.

"You got what you came for?" Victor asked.

Jeremy nodded. "I did indeed. You neither confirmed nor denied my suspicion as to what your thoughts are concerned with."

"Yes," Victor admitted, trying to keep his ire out of his voice. "I'm thinking about Rolf."

"And you are smart to do so," Jeremy said, his voice becoming harder, "he is not one to take lightly. I am sure you would rather be in Massachusetts, hunting him down. I assure you, Victor, that he is not forgotten. We will find him again, and we will stop him. But for right now it is too dangerous for me to leave you with him, and young Grant here is in jeopardy."

"The doll's in his apartment," Victor snapped, "how is that him being in jeopardy? Sounds more like he's put out for a bit. This couldn't have waited?"

"I don't think I can explain it well enough for you," Jeremy said, sighing, "but I wanted to visit my old friend anyway. She will explain the situation for you, and for Grant. Leanne Le Monde has a much better way with words than I do."

Victor shook his head, reluctant to let the subject go, but he did anyway.

"Do we need a cab?" he asked.

Both Grant and Jeremy nodded, with Jeremy saying, "Yes. Normally even I would attempt the walk, but not with my recent purchase."

Victor flagged down a cab, and as the vehicle pulled up to the curb, he glanced over his shoulder and asked, "What did you buy?"

"A coffin," Grant said as Victor opened the door for him. "He bought a child's coffin."

Surprised, Victor stared at Jeremy as the older man climbed into the back seat.

Jeremy gave him a small, tired smile and said, "You use the tool necessary for the job, Victor. Whatever that tool might be."

Victor said nothing as he got into the cab and reflected on what horrific tools Jeremy might have used in his life.

Chapter 37: Reprimanded

The house shook, and Stefan was thrown from his bed, landing on the floor hard enough to rattle his teeth and knock the wind out of him. Gasping for air with his head spinning from the pain, Stefan pushed himself into a sitting position.

Another violent tremor rippled through the house. Items fell and crashed, and the dead raised their voices in a cacophony of protest.

Stefan's father bellowed in Russian, and the spirits fell silent.

Ivan Korzh was still to be respected, regardless of his imprisonment.

Pressing his hands against his temples, Stefan attempted to get the pain in his jaw under control.

"Stefan Ivanovich Korzh!" his father yelled.

All of Stefan's pain was forgotten as he scrambled to his feet.

He too feared his father. The seals on the door might hold his father's dead back, but they were nothing to Ivan Korzh if the man chose to shatter them.

Stumbling and staggering in the darkness, fear forced Stefan to make his way to the door, calling out, "I am coming, Father!"

The house was silent around him as the dead listened and waited, longing to know why Ivan had destroyed the peace.

Stefan reached the door and came to a stop a few feet away, the pain creeping back into his thoughts as he stared at the portal, waiting.

"I am here, Father," Stefan said.

"You are a fool!" his father snarled.

Stefan recoiled, the words harsh and unforgiving, the old, untamable fear of childhood rearing its head. "Why?"

"You," Ivan hissed through the door, "did not retrieve your mother's prizes. And I have learned that you sent out more. More! How many of them did you scatter to the winds? You are supposed to be protecting them! They are your birthright!"

Stefan's thoughts spun, whirling through his mind. He tried to make sense of what his father meant, but he could not.

The sound of his father's enraged voice robbed him of his adulthood and made a cringing child of him once more.

"I don't understand," Stefan replied, reluctance thick in his voice.

"Of course you don't," grumbled his father. "You never paid attention to what your mother and I attempted to teach you. No, you joined the army and sought to battle the world, and not to gather the dead to you, as was our task."

Stefan bristled at the reprimand, at the slight against his military service. It was the one aspect of his life that he was proud of. The only portion of it that had provided him with skills he felt was useful, as the death of Aldo Collier had proven.

When his father spoke again, there was less anger in the man's voice.

"Oh, Stefanushka," his father said. "How many items have you sent out?"

Stefan almost replied that he didn't know, but his father would sense the lie. "Thirty-seven so far."

For several seconds his father didn't reply, and Stefan could picture the man when he had still been alive, how the color would drain from his face as the rage built.

"Thirty-seven," Ivan Korzh whispered, and then the entire house shook. It felt as though a giant reached down from the heavens and grabbed hold of the building and attempted to wrestle it free of its foundation.

The motion was violent enough to knock Stefan down. Screams erupted from the ghosts, and his father's dead howled with glee from their prison.

"If he has not yet identified the German in the bear as having been your mother's," his father hissed, "then he will make the connection soon enough. And if he should learn of Anne, then he will know without a doubt where they are coming from. You need to get them back. All of them. Each and every one you have sent out."

Stefan ignored the command. Those thirty-seven were only the first wave. The others would go out eventually, regardless of what his father wished.

Stefan tried to speak and gasped, the pain in his jaw excruciating. Finally, he managed to ask, "Who? Who are you talking about?"

"A man," his father snapped, "He will be older now. His body weakened. But if his mind is still as sharp as it was before, if his eyes still see the possessed, then you will be in a difficult position, my son."

Stefan grumbled and said, "I'll kill him."

Ivan let out a sharp, bitter laugh. "You will try, Stefanushka, you will try. What you must know, however, is that many others tried. He is stronger than you would suspect. And he will kill you as well."

It was Stefan's turn to laugh. "No, he'll not kill me, Father."

"What makes you think so?" Ivan asked in a soft voice.

"I'm a trained killer," Stefan said with pride, "and I am your son."

"That you are," Ivan said, "and it would be a pity for you to die at the hands of the same man who killed me."

Stefan started to respond, then realized what his father had said, and that there was nothing more to say.

Chapter 38: A Visit to an Old Friend

Leanne Le Monde was far older than anyone possibly imagined. They would not have believed her if she told them, but she had no intention of sharing that information either. She suspected that of all those who knew her, Mr. Jeremy Rhinehart might have a fair idea of her true age.

But he was far too much the gentleman to inquire as to the exact number of years she has been upon the planet.

Which was one of the many reasons why she enjoyed his company. On the few trips out of Louisiana, she always made a point to see where he happened to be in the world, and if he was close enough, they got together.

When the doorbell rang in the early evening, she half suspected it was Grant and his newest haunted item on her stoop again.

She was partly correct.

Grant was there, although he was thankfully without the second haunted item he had purchased. Leanne bristled at the sight of him, not wanting the foolishness that was sure to spew from his mouth.

Along with Grant was Jeremy Rhinehart, and another man she did not know. There was a look of sadness about the second man, as though his world had been turned upside down and gutted.

"Jeremy," she said with a smile, "I'm surprised to see you here."

"It was an unplanned adventure, my dear Miss Le Monde," Jeremy replied, smiling. "I was wondering if perhaps you would let us in?"

Leanne hesitated before she said, "I'm leery of the company you have with you, Jeremy. Young Grant here has made several foolish decisions and I would hate for them to follow him into my home."

"I understand," Jeremy said, "but we are here, upon his request and your recommendation, and I know that without your assistance in this matter we will not succeed."

Leanne nodded and stepped aside, opening the door wide for the man. "Your hip still bothers you?"

"It does, I am afraid," he said as he took her hand, bowed over it, and brushed her skin lightly with his lips. "You are looking as refined and as elegant as ever, Miss Le Monde."

"If I did not know you better, Jeremy," she said, chuckling, "I would call you a rake."

"Perhaps you should," Jeremy said. "You know Grant, but you do not know my young friend. This is Victor Daniels."

"A pleasure to meet you," Victor said, his voice reflecting the pain on his face.

"Come in, all of you," she said, stepping aside. "I see you've acquired a coffin?"

Grant looked at her in surprise, but Jeremy only let out a small laugh. "I am afraid it was the only lead-lined container to be found this evening on short notice."

"That is always an issue," she said, leading them into her sitting room and motioning for them to sit down. "Tea or coffee?"

"If it is already on," Jeremy said, answering for the others, "but if not then do not put yourself out."

"There is no trouble over tea or coffee," Leanne said. "I prepared a pot of tea a short while ago. It should still be fresh, and strong."

"Then please, we would all enjoy a cup," Jeremy replied.

Leanne nodded, retired to the kitchen, and made up a tray. Soon she returned to the sitting room and served the men their tea. When she sat down, she picked up her own cup, looked at them each in turn and said, "Tell me, Jeremy, are you here for Anne?"

Jeremy nodded. "I am. And I have a question for you, is it Anne Le Morte?"

"Of course it is," Leanne answered in a low voice, "and I know because of the song she sang."

Jeremy shot a sharp glance at Grant. "You did not tell me she was singing."

"I didn't think it was important," Grant said defensively.

"Your weakness is your lack of thinking," Leanne reprimanded. "The dead are nothing to be played with. They are real and powerful. Would you be so careless with a loaded pistol?"

"How are they even the same?" Grant snapped.

"They are not," Jeremy said in a voice etched with bitterness. "They are worse. You would be safer playing Russian roulette, especially with the likes of Anne Le Morte. She vanished from the collection circuit decades ago. I had hoped she would remain gone, but it seems as though it was an exercise in futility."

Jeremy turned his attention to Leanne and said, "I want to tell you that Rolf has been freed."

The name took Leanne by surprise, and she blinked several times as she regained her composure.

"The last I knew of Rolf," she said, "was that he had been purchased by Nicole Korzh. I do not believe she would part with him."

"I know she wouldn't," Jeremy said. "I attempted to obtain him decades ago and failed. I was wondering if you might know where Anne Le Morte had finally called home."

Leanne finished her tea, set the cup down, and said, "I do, as it happens. Ivan Denisovich acquired her."

She watched Jeremy's shoulders sag, and she felt pity for the man.

"Who is Ivan Denisovich?" Victor asked, looking from Leanne to Jeremy.

Leanne answered the question.

"Ivan Denisovich Korzh was the husband of Nicole," she explained. "He often went only by Ivan Denisovich, in honor of his father. Mr. Korzh was a collector of note, as was his wife. They specialized in violent items. His particular focus was on brutal murderers while Nicole's tended to be the insane and those who killed more of by accident than intent. It was rumored that they were hoarders of possessed objects. Their collection numbered in the hundreds."

"I had feared that Nicole's collection had been purloined," Jeremy said, straightening up, "and that perhaps the thief would sell them off one by one."

"But," Leanne said, continuing the narrative, "since know that at least one item is from Nicole's, and I suspect the other is Ivan's given its violent nature, we must accept the fact that the whole of both collections have been obtained."

"Hoarders don't give their belongings away," Grant said, "I know, my mother was a hoarder; she left everything to me when she passed."

Leanne nodded. "You are quite correct, young man. They don't give them away."

"There was a rumor," Jeremy said, "many, many years ago, that the Korzhs had a child. Yet whether that child was a male or female, I do not know. It would seem though that he has inherited his parents' belongings. Which would include the deadliest collection of possessed items that I know of."

"Yes," Leanne said in agreement. "The question now, gentlemen, is what shall we do about it."

"All I want is my home back," Grant said, a note of fear in his voice. "I regret ever having ordered Anne."

"That is not the only item you ordered, is it?" Leanne asked coldly.

He shook his head.

"What else did you purchase from the seller?" Jeremy asked. "I do not recall that you ever told me."

"A teapot," Grant said, clearing his throat. "A Wedgwood teapot."

Leanne watched as Jeremy's eyes narrowed and he inquired, "For a doll, or full sized?"

"Doll," Grant answered.

"Where is it?" Jeremy demanded. "Where have you left it?"

"In my apartment building," Grant said, looking confused. "It's in the box, by my door. I thought I could bring it in when we went to get Anne."

"How long ago was that?" Jeremy asked.

"Only a little while before I left to pick you up at the airport," Grant explained.

"What is it?" Victor asked.

"If it is the teapot we fear it is," Jeremy said, nodding to Leanne, "then it needs to be recovered immediately."

"Why?" Grant asked. "It was only supposed to be a little haunted."

"The child who owned it before," Jeremy explained through clenched teeth, "poisoned a string of nannies with mercury before they finally realized what she was doing."

"I don't see what the problem is," grumbled Grant. "It's in the damned box still."

"Fool!" Jeremy hissed. "Do you think that's going to stop her? Did Anne being in a closed room stop her?"

Grant's face paled as he shook his head.

"I will call you a cab," Leanne said, getting to her feet. "I am sorry your visit here has to be under such circumstances, Mr. Rhinehart."

Jeremy gave her a tight smile. "I feel the same, Miss Le Monde. For far too long I have been away from the French Quarter."

"He's dead you know," Leanne said, smiling. "Old Father Grosbec."

"I know," Jeremy said, "unfortunately his warning is not."

She let out a mirthless laugh and went to call them a cab, fearful she was sending her friend to his death.

Chapter 39: Mrs. Ducharme and the Cold

Nina Ducharme had lived her entire life in the city of New Orleans. Only recently had her son moved her to the upscale apartment building located far from the neighborhoods with which she was familiar. Each day she made her way to the local markets, purchased her food for the evening meal, and made certain to stop at the cemetery to wish her husband well. He had been a miserable man in life, but he had always loved her.

When the elevator doors opened, and she stepped onto her floor, she shuddered. A blast of cold air slapped the breath out of her mouth and left her cheeks stinging.

Muttering against the incompetency of the building's superintendent, Nina made her way towards her apartment. She reached into her purse, retrieved her keys, and her cold fingers promptly dropped them.

It was as she bent down to retrieve them that she saw the package in front of Grant's door. The cardboard was small, and it had been opened, and she knew it had not been done so by her neighbor. He often received packages, but he never allowed them to sit out overnight, and he certainly would not have opened it and left it there, half propped against his door.

I should seal that for him, she thought, picking up her keys. As she straightened up the fob with the picture of her two smiling grandchildren clacked against the buckle of her purse. Absently, she put the keys into her pocket and walked over to the package. Nina picked it up, the cardboard cold and rough in her hands.

Yes, she thought, carrying it back to her own apartment, *I'll bring it in. But I should make certain nothing inside is broken before I seal it. Grant would be terribly upset if what he ordered had been broken or damaged in some way.*

Nina nodded to herself, managed to retrieve her keys with success, and let herself into the apartment. Her cat, Mr. Tabby, wandered out to see her, but when his orange eyes lighted upon the box, his ears flattened against his skull. A low, mewling growl came rumbling out of his throat as the hair on his spine rose up.

Surprised, Nina watched as the cat arched his back, then turned and fled from the room.

With a shrug, she carried the box to the dining table, set it down and turned to find the tape.

She hesitated, then sat down at the table instead.

Nina lowered the box onto its side, reached in and found a shipping manifest. On it she read, *One doll-sized Wedgwood Teapot, Haunted. $300.*

She smiled at the thought of Grant buying an item as frivolous as a teapot for a doll when he didn't have any daughters or nieces. Perhaps it was the idea of the Wedgwood being haunted that had enticed him.

Might as well see what a haunted teapot looks like, she thought. Nina reached in, took out several sheets of bubble wrap, then touched the graceful, unique finish of a piece of genuine Wedgwood. She withdrew it carefully and sighed with appreciation when it was free of the box.

The Wedgewood was done in Jasper Blue, a pattern she loved. Roman ladies were seated on divans while servants filled their cups from tall wine jars.

As Nina turned the piece in her hands, enjoying the feel of it against her fingers, she realized she had never had tea from a Wedgwood teapot before. A curious sensation stole over her, as if her thoughts were being guided by an unseen hand.

Then she smiled and wondered if it would taste better than tea from an average receptacle. Nina understood she would never have another chance to drink from such an item.

She knew, too, that Grant wouldn't mind. Not at all. He would want her to have tea. Nina was sure he would even thank her for making sure the tea steeped properly in Wedgwood.

She would, in fact, be doing him a considerable favor. And he was always so kind and considerate, helping her whenever she needed it.

How could I do anything less than try the teapot for him?

Excited, Nina stood up and brought the pot into the kitchen. She found herself whistling as she went about setting some water to boil. It was an old song, one she hadn't thought of since she was a little girl and enjoying her first Mardi Gras.

Nina took down a strong black tea, spooned some out into an infuser and set it aside. Still whistling, she left the kitchen for the bathroom and opened the medicine cabinet. She rummaged around in it until she found what she wanted, then brought it back with her to the kitchen. The water had begun to whistle in the kettle, and she transferred it to the teapot.

Nina took up the infuser, lowered it into the hot water, and then picked up the item she had retrieved from the bathroom.

It was an old thermometer. She had used it on her children when they were young. It was made of glass and the red line within was filled with mercury.

Nina snapped off the bulb end of the thermometer and let the contents spill into the hot water. When she was sure that the last drop had found its way into the teapot, she put the thermometer in the trash and waited for the tea to steep.

Whistling, Nina carried the teapot and a teacup back to the table. She sat down, poured herself a cup, and smiled at the little girl who sat across from her.

What a pretty child, Nina thought as she took her first sip.

A moment later, she let out a happy laugh, and the child joined in.

The tea did taste better from a Wedgwood teapot.

With the little girl clapping her hands, Nina drained the cup.

Chapter 40: Grant's Building

When the elevator doors opened, Victor gasped, the cold air sharp and painful to inhale.

Beside him, Grant shrank back against the sidewall, his eyes widening.

Their breath tumbled out of their mouths and nostrils in great, billowing clouds and Jeremy shook his head as he stepped out into the hall. He leaned on his cane and glanced back at Grant who continued to cower.

"Which door is yours, young man?" Jeremy asked.

"The one on the right," Grant answered.

"Who lives in the left-hand apartment?" Victor asked, noticing that the door to that suite was ajar.

"Mrs. Ducharme," Grant said, taking a nervous step away from the wall as Victor reached out a hand and kept the elevator doors open. "Where's the package?"

Jeremy gave the man a disgusted look, snapping, "It would seem as though your neighbor has found the package."

"She wouldn't touch it," Grant protested. "She's not nosy."

"It doesn't matter," Jeremy said. "Not in the least. Are you really so foolish to think that someone is in complete control of their faculties around one of the dead who is as powerful as these?"

Grant didn't answer, turning his gaze to the floor instead.

Victor bent down and picked up the paper wrapped coffin. It was heavy in his arms, and he understood why Grant had set it down to begin with. Victor held onto it as he hurried after Jeremy, who was marching toward Mrs. Ducharme's apartment.

When he reached it, he hesitated, lifted his cane, and prodded the door open.

Grant let out a high-pitched scream as an orange cat barreled out of the apartment, sprinting for the safety of a potted plant by the elevator.

Jeremy stepped into the doorway but did not cross the threshold. He shook his head and shot an angry look at Grant.

"This," Jeremy said in disgust, "is on you."

Victor and Grant reached the door at the same time, peering around Jeremy to see what he was referring to.

Grant turned away first, stumbling towards the elevator, and making it half way before he fell onto his hands and knees and began to vomit.

An old woman, still wearing a coat and with her groceries on the dining table, sat in a chair, her torso and head on the wood top. Blood and bile were spread out around and beneath her. A teapot made for a doll stood on the table near her.

Victor watched as Jeremy used the handle of his cane to hook the edge of the door and pull it closed. He snapped around and faced Grant, who sat in silence on the floor. The entire hall stank of vomit and Victor wondered in a detached way what the man could have eaten that smelled so badly.

"Did you see her?" Jeremy demanded.

Grant nodded and kept his eyes averted.

"You are at fault," he spat, pointing his cane at the man. "Yours, and yours alone. If you had taken care with the package, she would not have been placed in such a situation. Few can resist the charms of the dead."

"I didn't know," Grant protested.

"Then you should have educated yourself prior to doing something stupid!" Jeremy yelled. He seethed for a moment and then added, "Now I must retrieve the teapot. It needs to be done quickly, else Anne will hear."

Grant stiffened at the doll's name.

Jeremy gave him a curt nod. "You're right to be afraid. The locked door won't stop her now. Can't you feel the power here? You must sense it."

Victor shook his head, saying, "No, Jeremy, I can't. I'm sorry."

Jeremy relaxed at Victor's statement and then patted the younger man on the arm. He focused on Grant once more.

"Do you think you have the courage to enter your own home with us?" Jeremy asked.

Grant hesitated, then nodded. His face was set in a rigid mask of fear, but there was the glint of determination in his eyes.

Victor admired the man, in spite of his foolishness with regards to the haunted doll. Grant didn't have to go into the apartment. He had no personal stake in it. The man had not lost his wife or any loved one.

A deep hate smoldered in Victor, and he looked forward to the day when he could punish the man who had set the likes of Rolf and Anne on the world.

"Victor," Jeremy said, "will you help me here?"

He nodded.

"I am going to open the door in a moment, and we will have to look upon the dead Mrs. Ducharme," Jeremy explained. "If we are fortunate we will not have to see anyone else."

"Alright," Victor said, swallowing a dry lump in his throat. "What do you need me to do?"

"You will carry the coffin and open it for me. I will pick up the teapot and place it in the coffin. At that time you will close it, and we will back out of the apartment, post haste," Jeremy said with a tight smile.

Grant, who seemed to have gotten grasp of his fear, straightened up and said, "Sounds pretty straight forward."

"It does," Jeremy agreed, "and it never is."

Grant blanched and cast his gaze to Victor.

Victor shrugged and said, "Since you're not going in with us, maybe you could keep an eye on your apartment door and make sure Anne doesn't come out to say hello."

Without waiting to hear Grant's response, Victor tore the paper off the coffin, seeing the object for the first time.

It was brilliant and beautiful, and utterly depressing all in one heartbreaking moment. The sides and lid were made of faceted glass, each pane set into beautifully wrought brass. It could not have measured more than two feet in length, less than half of that in width and depth. The interior held what looked to be a satin pillow and bedding of the same material. There were stains upon all of it, and Victor had the terrible suspicion that the coffin had at one time been used. Where the original occupant had gone to, and what had become of the child's remains, could only be surmised.

"Best not to think about it," Jeremy said in a soft voice. "There is nothing of the child here. The spirit has moved on. This is nothing more than glass and metal. Lead keeps the glass in place and serves as a buffer between the upper and lower parts. It will keep the dead trapped within it."

Victor could only nod, remembering the hopes Erin had once harbored for children of their own.

"Grant," Jeremy said, "watch your door, as Victor suggested, and get us immediately if you even suspect the doorknob of beginning to turn."

Grant nodded, wide-eyed, and fixed his gaze on the door in question.

"Are you ready, Victor?" Jeremy asked.

Victor snorted a laugh, shook his head, and said, "No."

"You're a wise man," Jeremy said, turning back to Mrs. Ducharme's door. "Let us hope that this next task can go as smoothly as possible."

Hope in one hand, spit in the other, Victor thought as the older man reached for the doorknob, *and let's see what fills up quicker.*

The door swung wide, and a little girl smiled at them before she slammed it closed.

Chapter 41: Unwelcomed and Unwanted

Jeremy shook his head at the door as he took out a pair of white, cotton gloves from a pocket and pulled them on. He made certain they were on securely, sighed and reached out for the knob. His hand passed through a wall of cold, the metal painful to the touch even through the fabric as he grasped it. Clenching his teeth, Jeremy gave the knob a sharp turn and forced the door open.

His eyes darted around the room, ignoring the teapot on the table in front of the dead woman.

When he didn't see the little girl, he fixed his attention on the Wedgwood, letting his gaze go out of focus as he did so. In a heartbeat, he saw her, off to the left, pressed close to the wall as she watched him.

"Victor," Jeremy said, "I want you to stay close to me, and to look only at me. Nothing else. No matter what you hear. Do you understand?"

"I do," Victor answered, and Jeremy was impressed with the strength he heard in the younger man's voice.

Jeremy took a deep, measured breath and advanced towards the table.

The girl took a small step away from the wall, anger and curiosity warring for domination of her expression.

Anger won out.

"Get away from there!" she shouted, and all of the glass exploded in the picture frames on the walls.

Jeremy ignored her and continued towards the table.

"Stop him!" the girl shrieked, and the corpse at the table jerked upright.

Victor gasped behind him, and Jeremy could only hope the man would do as he had bidden him.

Mrs. Ducharme's face was twisted and pressed against itself, a Salvador Dali impersonation of humanity. The stench of death rolled off her, the putrid scent of bile and sickness permeating the air.

"Get him, now!" the little girl commanded, and Mrs. Ducharme got to her feet.

She tottered towards Jeremy, and while she shambled like a zombie from a B movie, he knew she was dangerous. Her strength would be terrific, and he would be little match for her.

So when she was close enough, he lifted his cane and lashed out with it. The blow caught her in the head and caused her to stumble. He reversed the swing of it, brought the cane back, and hooked her ankle with the handle. With a grunt, he pulled up and took her feet out from under her.

The dead woman landed with a crash that shook the teapot on the table and caused the teacup to roll onto the floor.

Howling with fury, the little girl charged at him.

Yet Jeremy had been waiting for her to do exactly that, and when she reached him, Jeremy lashed out with the cane.

A triumphant grin appeared on her face, but it vanished along with her.

"Quickly, Victor!" Jeremy shouted, stepping over Mrs. Ducharme's corpse and hurrying to the table. He ignored the pain that shot through his fingers as he snatched up the teapot and spun around.

Victor, pale faced but steady, held the coffin open, and Jeremy dropped the offensive piece of Wedgwood in. With a snap, Victor closed the lid, secured the lock, and let out a long, shuddering breath.

A glance at the floor showed that Mrs. Ducharme was indeed nothing more than a corpse again.

"Jeremy," Victor said.

"Hm?" he replied, taking a deep breath and letting it out slowly.

"That was terrible," Victor said.

Jeremy nodded his head in agreement, adding, "And it is only going to get worse. Now we need to see Anne."

As the name left his lips, he heard Grant scream from the corridor.

Chapter 42: Not Seeing Things

Grant's scream stopped as the doorknob to his apartment completed its turn, the click of the catch loud and frightening in the sudden stillness of the corridor. The door opened inch by inch, stopping and starting as it revealed the darkness of his home beyond.

A heartbeat later, a small doll's hand reached around the edge of the wooden portal, grasped it with porcelain fingers that creaked and groaned, and tugged the door open the rest of the way.

Anne Le Morte stood on the threshold, framed by the deep black of the apartment, and a sigh of happiness escaped her and washed over Grant.

She spoke to him in French, rapidly fired words with a lilt both beautiful and frightening. His stomach turned and clenched, threatening to push the last vestiges of food up his throat.

By the elevator, the tabby cat that had escaped from Mrs. Ducharme's apartment let out a long howl of fear and desperation that Grant empathized with.

Grant opened his mouth to speak, but only a small, pitiful moan escaped his lips.

Victor stepped out of Mrs. Ducharme's apartment, the coffin in his hand. Jeremy stepped out behind him, the older man's face showing signs of exhaustion.

Anne pointed a finger at Jeremy, snarling as she spoke.

Jeremy shook his head, responding, "Mademoiselle Anne Le Morte, I am afraid I do not speak your patois. Or any French, really."

The doll's face twisted into a grimace, flakes of porcelain dropping to the floor.

By the elevator, the cat meowed again, and Anne's head snapped to look at the animal.

A low, guttural sound came from the doll and Grant looked at the cat.

From the feline's throat came a strangled shriek as the pet was lifted up by an unseen hand.

Before any of them could react, the cat's protest was cut short by a loud snap, its body going limp.

"Oh my God," Grant whispered, then he recoiled and tried to shrink within himself as the cat flew down the corridor and smashed into the back of his head.

The blow knocked him to the carpet, and Anne's strange, high laugh filled the room.

She spoke in French to Jeremy again, but the old man's response was to Victor, not the doll.

"Are you ready again?" Jeremy asked.

"Sure," Victor said, his voice small, "why not. This one's even worse, isn't she?"

"She certainly is," Jeremy agreed. "But that doesn't make her invincible."

Fighting back the rising terror, Grant struggled to get to his feet. But as he gathered himself together, Anne raced toward him. Paralyzed with fear, Grant found he couldn't move as she neared him.

Victor could.

Still holding the child-sized coffin in his arms, he sprang forward, lashing out with a foot that caught Anne squarely in the stomach.

The doll flew backward from the force of the blow, passing over the threshold and landing with a crash in Grant's apartment. He felt an absurd desire to yell out, *Goal!* But he restrained himself, biting his tongue until it bled.

Anne reappeared a second later, screaming at them all.

The walls of the corridor shook, and the lights above them flickered and popped.

They were left in complete darkness.

Above the sound of his own ragged breathing, Grant heard two noises.

The first was the patter of Anne's feet on the floor.

And the second was that of a long, drawn out scream which he realized wasn't hers, but his own.

Chapter 43: The Battle in the Corridor

Jeremy, Victor decided, was prepared for every eventuality.

Within seconds of the lights having been put out in the corridor, the older man had cracked several glow sticks, their combined glow illuminating the doll.

She was terrifying.

Victor and Jeremy moved towards Grant, who lay prostrate with fear on the floor. Yet even as they did so, Anne raced towards them, her small legs moving terrifyingly fast. As she neared them Jeremy swung his cane, and to Victor's surprise, the doll dodged it, as though she had expected the attack.

Again and again, Jeremy lashed out at her but her quick, deft movements kept her free from harm even as Victor and Jeremy attempted to do the same for Grant.

"Grant," Victor snapped, "get up!"

The only response he received from the other man was a pathetic moan.

Then, Anne darted in between all of them, reaching out and grasping a full chunk of Grant's hair in her porcelain hand while racing by. The man's head snapped back, bloody foam spilling out of the corners of his mouth as his eyes flicked madly from left to right in opposite directions.

He was twisted around and would have gone further if his hair hadn't suddenly torn free from his scalp, leaving her with a bloody clump.

Anne let out a high, pleased laugh and ran into the apartment.

She left the door open.

Victor tried to take hold of Grant's arm and the man scrambled away from him, crawling on all fours toward the elevator.

"Don't worry about him," Jeremy said coldly. "We have to contend with Anne. He is on his own."

Before Victor could respond, Anne raced out of the apartment, something bright glistening in her hands.

Jeremy lunged, struck her hand with his cane, and fell to the floor, landing with a loud thud as a piece of broken glass spun out of her hand. Somehow, the man managed to keep the doll in the light of the glow sticks.

The doll let out an invective in French and came to a sharp stop, turning her attention to Jeremy, who was open to attack on the floor.

"Don't," Victor said, stepping towards her. "Don't even think about it."

"Be careful," Jeremy said, his voice tight with pain.

A loud bang sounded, and all eyes turned to the elevator, where Grant had pulled himself up and had begun to pound on the metal doors.

Anne laughed and sped towards the man.

Grant twisted around, a fresh scream exploding from his throat as he saw the doll. He clawed at the carpet, trying to dig his way into it.

Victor put the coffin down as quickly as he could without shattering it and ran after Anne. While his stride was longer, she had too much of a lead on him, and she reached Grant first.

The man threw his hands up in front of him, protecting his face, but the doll took aim at his groin. She stamped down with a small foot, and the piercing shriek that launched itself from his lips caused Victor to wince.

As he neared her, the doll's blows continued to land with precision and ferocity.

Victor heard Grant's teeth break and jaw snap. Flesh was torn from one cheek, and two fingers were mangled. When Victor reached them, Anne had taken Grant's chin in one hand, and before she could be stopped, the doll plunged her free hand deep into the man's left eye.

She jerked it back, pulling the mangled orb with her as he slumped to the floor, passed out from the pain. The doll faced Victor, squeezed the plucked eye into jelly and let it drip from her fingers.

In a soft, sweet voice, she asked him a question in French.

"I don't know what you want," Victor replied, "and I don't care."

He stepped up to the doll and ignored Jeremy as the man shouted, "Stop, Victor!"

There was pain when he grabbed a fistful of the doll's hair and lifted her up. It felt as if he had thrust his hand into a bucket of dry ice and every second he held onto her the sensation worsened.

Anne laughed again, swinging merrily by her locks. Her mirth ended when she discovered Victor still held on in spite of the pain.

She screamed at him in French, kicked out and tried to grab his hand. But her hair was too long and her arms too short. She could no more force him to let go than she could take a breath of air.

Victor gasped, sucked in breath through teeth clenched against the pain and focused on the coffin. Yet as his eyes locked onto it, the temperature plummeted and Jeremy's glow stick suddenly dimmed. The corridor was plunged into almost pure darkness, the fading glow sticks adding nothing more than a hint of light.

"What do you think that did, Anne Le Morte?" grumbled Victor. "I can still see where your coffin is."

"Walk quickly," Jeremy called. "You'll lose your hand if you don't."

Victor heard the sound of someone scrambling on the floor, a sound swiftly followed by the click of the coffin lid as Jeremy unlocked it.

Anne howled with fury, jerking her entire body to either side. She tried to free herself from Victor's grasp, but he had no intention of releasing her. The French that spewed forth from her mouth sounded like a recording sped up. Grant let out a scream, the pain of his wound registering and waking him.

"Ignore it all," Jeremy said as Victor drew closer, the glow sticks flickering their dim, fading light across the floor "Worry only about coming to the coffin."

Victor struck an object with his foot, and Jeremy let out a gasp of pain.

"You're here, Victor," the older man hissed, "just put her in the coffin now. If that was your foot, then you're less than a foot away."

Victor didn't have time to respond. Objects struck him in the small of the back while several glanced off the side of his head. He knew the door to Grant's apartment was behind him, and Anne was launching household items at him.

Glass shattered, and furniture crashed. A heavy object clipped the back of his skull and caused him to stumble as stars exploded in front of his eyes.

"Find the coffin!" Jeremy commanded.

Victor obeyed and dropped to his knees. His free hand found the cold metal and glass of the coffin, and he lifted the lid. The girl from Mrs. Ducharme's apartment let out a foul litany of curses as he thrust Anne into the receptacle. As he extricated his hand, both the doll and the girl attacked him and it felt as though thousands of needles were buried into the tender flesh of his palm and the skin between his fingers.

Letting out a shout of dismay, Victor fell back, the lid dropping back into place with a large clack.

He lay on his back, warmth returning to the corridor. His hand was an agonized mass of punished flesh, and he wondered if he would ever be able to use it again.

The groans and whimpers issuing from Grant were clear and aggravating in the darkness. There was a scrape and a hiss as Jeremy moved. Victor listened as the man locked the coffin and then sighed.

"Victor," Jeremy said, "are you alright?"

He laughed and shook his head as he said, "No. Not at all."

"I thought not," Jeremy said.

"I'm pretty sure I'm going to pass out," Victor said, the pain spreading from his hand up to his forearm, tendrils of the same burning along his nerves towards his elbow.

"Well, before you do that, I wanted to make one statement," Jeremy said.

"Go for it," Victor said, wincing against the growing pain.

"Well done, my friend," Jeremy said. "Well done."

"Thanks," Victor managed, and then he closed his eyes against the pain and consciousness.

Chapter 44: An Unfortunate Phone Call

Grant had been admitted to the hospital and Jeremy had gone to see Leanne Le Monde. Victor was still in a suite in the ER, his hand being treated for severe frostbite.

A pale blue curtain separated him from the hub of the emergency room, and a pair of white running shoes appeared beneath the hem of it. The curtain was pushed aside by a middle-aged woman, her hair pulled back into a tight ponytail. She wore a pair of rimless glasses, and her face was angular, sharp and barren of any makeup. Her nametag read, *Dr. Elizabeth Stowe.*

"Mr. Daniels," she said, her words spoken with a curious lilt that hinted at a childhood in a country other than America. "Tell me, how does one manage to sustain a frostbite injury in New Orleans?"

"That's an excellent question," he replied, "and it deserves an equally fantastic answer."

She waited, tapping her fingers on a clipboard.

"Mr. Daniels," Dr. Stowe said after a moment, "do you have an answer for me?"

"None that you would believe or accept," he stated, "that would not result in me being placed into protective custody for an undetermined amount of time."

"Does that mean I should commit you?" she asked.

"Not at all," he responded. "Now, if you would kindly discharge me, Doctor, I would appreciate it."

"And what of your friend?" Dr. Stowe asked, glancing down at her notes, "What of Grant Ross?"

Victor shrugged as he answered, "I believe Mr. Ross is an adult, Doctor, and he will be fine. I will, of course, check in on him later on. But, as they say, he's a big boy."

"Mr. Daniels," she said in a voice brimming with anger, "your friend has suffered a debilitating injury to his reproductive organs. Someone tore out an eye. He is currently unconscious and unable to answer any of our questions, so I am asking you, before I bring in the police, to tell me what happened to both of you."

Victor examined her, saw there was no bluff in her eyes, and said, "We entered his apartment. On his floor, we stepped out of the elevator, and I don't remember anything else."

Her lips formed a thin line as she shook her head, spun around on her heel and left the room.

In less than a minute, a young male nurse entered the room. He had a confused expression on his face, and he carried a portable phone.

"Mr. Daniels," the young man said, "you have a phone call."

Frowning, Victor accepted the phone with his uninjured hand.

"Yes?" he asked.

"Mr. Daniels," a woman said, "this is Officer Lee of the Pepperell police department."

It took a moment for the name to register, and when it did, his brain accessed the memory of the night Sue Jeffries was murdered.

"Yes, Officer Lee," Victor said, remembering the police woman he had lied to, "this is a rather strange time for you to be calling me. And how did you know to call me here, in the hospital?"

"The New Orleans police department called about you," she replied and said no more on the subject.

He cleared his throat and asked, "To what do I owe the pleasure?"

"It is nothing good, I'm afraid," she said, sounding genuinely sympathetic. "Your house burned down last night."

Victor blinked, looked down at his lap and said, "I'm sorry. It sounds as if you said my house burned down."

"It did," Officer Lee continued, "and we were wondering when you might be returning to Pepperell from your New Orleans trip."

"I, well, I think tomorrow, perhaps the day after at the latest," Victor said, his thoughts spinning. "Why?"

"We need you to stop by the station when you get in," she answered, her voice pleasant. "We have some paperwork to go over with you. Nothing too drastic."

"Alright then," Victor said, still trying to come to grips with what the woman had told him. "I'll stop by as soon as I'm back."

"Great," she said, a happy tone in her voice, "we'll see you then."

The call ended and Victor was left with the phone pressed to his ear, the dial tone loud and penetrating.

Confused, Victor placed the phone on the bed, ignorant of the nurse, the room, his injured hand, and everything except the fact that his house had burned down.

Chapter 45: A Visit with Leanne

She had fixed him a cup of black tea laced with nutmeg.

Jeremy cradled the worn china cup in his hands, staring at the faint outline of the china's pattern on the interior of the vessel.

"Was she difficult?" Leanne asked.

Jeremy nodded, took a sip and said, "Very, I am afraid. She injured Grant."

"So I gathered," Leanne replied. "I called the hospital and made inquiries about his condition, and young Victor's as well."

"Victor did well," Jeremy said, focusing on her. "He was far better than I thought he would be. The man was unflappable, and for that, I am grateful. Anne would have had me otherwise."

Leanne walked to the coffin, which lay on the floor beneath a painting of a rose filled burial ground. Jeremy watched her as she stared down at the doll through the glass.

"Do you know her story, Jeremy?" Leanne asked before she turned around and went back to her chair.

He shook his head. "I know her name. I know what she has done since occupying the doll, but other than that, I know nothing."

"She was the daughter of a poor farmer," Leanne said. "A local businessman felt a fatherly affection for her since she reminded him of his own daughter, who had passed away years earlier. She thought that if the businessman became her father, then she would have more dolls."

Leanne paused before she continued.

"Soon, there was tragedy at her home. People believed that her mother killed her father, then herself, leaving Anne an orphan at the age of seven. Later, much later in life, after Anne died, it came to light that she had slain her parents, all in an effort to own more possessions."

"She was a murderer, even from a young age," Jeremy mused.

Leanne nodded.

"It should be no surprise that she managed to establish herself in the businessman's home. First, it was as a guest, but as she grew older, the man became enamored of her. His first wife passed away when she was thrown from a horse and died. A second wife followed, but she killed herself within a year of their marriage. These too, it would turn out, had been the work of Anne. She grew more cunning and deadly as she grew older."

"I surmise there was little that Anne balked at," Jeremy said, looking to Leanne.

She nodded, finished her own tea, hesitated, and then continued her tale.

"Within six months, she and the businessman were married. Five months after that, the first of three children were born," Leanne said, "and three were all God graced her with. While he made her fertile, he did not make her patient, nor did he make her pleasant. There is an article, from New Orleans, about how she murdered her husband and their sons. She had planned the death of the governess as well, but the girl got away and told the authorities. When the police arrived, she held onto her doll, and she had finished stitching the mouths of her kin shut. When the police tried to take her, she fought them until they were forced to kill her."

"She sounds," Jeremy said, "as if she were an absolute delight to know."

Leanne graced him with a crooked smile and said, "Evidently. Even with her crimes laid before the public, many of them still could not believe a woman of her beauty – and she was exceptionally beautiful – could be guilty of such crimes. She was a terrible fiend, Jeremy, and I am impressed with how you captured her."

"Well, as I said, my friend," Jeremy sighed, adjusting his position in the chair, "it was Victor who saved the day."

"Jeremy," Leanne said, frowning, "are you saying you did not place her in the coffin?"

"That is exactly what I am saying," Jeremy said, nodding. "Not only did he confine her, but he did so without the benefit of protection. He is at the hospital now, being treated for his injuries."

"He should not have survived," Leanne murmured, more to herself than to Jeremy. "Not with someone as powerful as she. Tell me, what do you know of him?"

"Nothing, when it comes down to it," Jeremy admitted. "I know his wife was slain by Rolf. I know the man seeks vengeance. Other than that, I do not even know what he does for work, his hobbies, or any single aspect of his past."

"You told me he is from Massachusetts," she said, tapping her fingers on her teacup. "And truly, I can hear his accent, but perhaps he was not born there."

"What are you thinking of, Leanne?" Jeremy asked, leaning forward. "Will you tell me?"

She shook her head and smiled. "The wandering thoughts of an old woman, Jeremy. Nothing more. But should you ask after his lineage, please, you will let me know the answer?"

Jeremy nodded, any words he might have spoken were cut off by the sudden ringing of his cellphone. He excused himself and answered the phone.

"Grant's awake," Victor said without preamble.

"Are you with him?" Jeremy asked.

"Yes," Victor sighed, "I am."

"Excellent," Jeremy said, "I'll be there shortly. We have to get the address from him in Commack."

"I know," Victor said, his voice cold. "I haven't forgotten."

"I didn't think you had," Jeremy said gently. "I will see you soon, Victor."

He ended the call and put the phone away as Leanne said, "Mr. Ross has awakened?"

"He has," Jeremy confirmed. "I will gain the address for the home in New York, and then Victor and I will attend to whoever is the possessor of the Korzh Collection."

"Be cautious," Leanne warned. "If it is indeed their child, then you will be approaching someone with all the wiles and skill of the parents."

"I will," Jeremy said, getting to his feet. "And I will be certain to have Victor be careful as well. Thank you for the tea, Leanne, and for the company."

She gave him a pleased smile and stood up to show him to the door.

When he stood on the street with the night sounds of New Orleans moving around him, Jeremy took a deep breath, hailed a taxi, and tried not to think of what might be waiting for them in New York.

Chapter 46: Unwelcome Company

Grant lay on the hospital bed, his thoughts blurred by the pain medication fed into his system by the IV bag which hung above him.

Victor and Jeremy stood at the end of his bed, backlit by the light of the corridor revealed by the room's open door. They had come for the address in New York, and he had given it to them. But as he lay on the bed, Grant had a difficult time focusing on them, not only from the medication but also because of his sudden lack of depth perception.

He tried to move in the bed, but the pain was instant and explosive, reminding him of the events in his apartment building.

His face must have shown his agony for Jeremy asked, "Is there anything I can do for you before we go?"

Grant had several angry retorts pass through his mind, but he swallowed back each of them. It hadn't been Jeremy or Victor who had purchased the doll, or the teapot. Nor had they forced him to go along with them to recover either of the items.

Grant was embarrassed, he realized, for the way he had acted. His desire to run away in spite of his efforts to stay and help shamed him.

He had proven himself to be nothing more than a base coward, and the presence of the two men at the foot of his hospital bed was a painful reminder of that.

As a young man, Grant had always fancied himself as brave and courageous, and as he aged, he had never come across someone who had challenged that belief. Anne Le Morte and the corpse of Mrs. Ducharme had not only challenged it, but shredded it and revealed it for the fallacy that it was.

"Where is the coffin?" Grant managed to ask. Not out of a desire to know its exact location, but rather to know he didn't have anything to fear from a vengeful ghost.

"With Miss Le Monde," Jeremy said. "She will keep it for me until I can have it brought to my own home in Norwich,

Connecticut. Once there, I will be able to keep both Anne and the ghost in the teapot contained."

"Are you going now?" Grant asked. "To Long Island?"

"Yes," Jeremy answered, "we cannot put it off any longer. The collection needs to be secured, and the sooner, the better. I am fearful of the harm that may have been wrought. I doubt only three were released into the wild as it were."

"Do you want us to tell you when it's over?" Victor asked.

"No," Grant snapped. Then he regained control and let out a strained sigh. "Yes. Please. I'll sleep better."

Jeremy and Victor were silent for a moment before the older man said, "Grant, you have my number. And you know how to contact Miss Le Monde. Do not hesitate to reach out to either one of us if you find you cannot sleep without the aid of narcotics or alcohol. There are people who can help you if you wish it."

Grant held back an angry retort, felt the first pangs that warned of the weakening of the painkiller's effectiveness, and muttered, "I will. But leave. Please. I can't see you. You remind me of her."

"Anne?" Victor asked.

Grant shook his head.

"Mrs. Ducharme," he whispered. "Mrs. Ducharme."

The two men left the room, abandoning Grant to his memories.

With a whimper, he found the call button for the nurse and pressed it.

He needed something, anything, to erase the image of Mrs. Ducharme's corpse. By the time the nurse came hurrying into the room, Grant was weeping, and there was nothing anyone could do.

Chapter 47: Waiting for the Trap to Spring

Stefan knew it was a stereotype, but he didn't care. He enjoyed the taste of vodka, and he never drank to excess.

His father had warned him of the dangers of that, and Stefan had witnessed it himself on more than one occasion. Neither of his parents had approved of his experiments, where he would bring a possessed item to a bar and allow it to run wild for a while.

Often the police became involved, an incident having occurred, and his father invariably found out about his extracurricular activities.

Stefan chuckled at the memories, poured himself a little more of the vodka, a brand named Tovaritch, and well worth the money he paid for it.

He put the bottle away and returned his attention to the monitor set up beside his laptop.

The new monitor was dedicated to the house in Commack in Long Island. He had gone back over the weekend and installed several cameras in the house, as well as four more around it. Stefan was able to view each and every aspect of the building, as well as the approaches to it. The system was also designed to alert him via text should he be away from the monitor.

But he had no intention of traveling any farther than down the hall to his bedroom. Soon, he suspected, someone would make an effort to enter the trap, and Stefan eagerly awaited the results.

Part of him was concerned that he hadn't done enough. There was a gnawing suspicion residing in his mind about whether or not his father had blown the situation out of proportion. Granted, Stefan had never seen his father even remotely concerned with regards to another collector before, but perhaps being dead had given him that which he lacked in life – fear of anything or anyone.

Yet his father had said the man in question had killed him and then gone silent on the subject. He had refused to utter the man's name or where he lived.

Stefan suspected the great Ivan Denisovich Korzh was still afraid of the man who had robbed him of life.

Curiously, Stefan felt no animosity towards the unnamed man. Stefan had never been exceptionally close with his father, or with his mother. Both of his parents had existed as peripherals in his life. They were there to provide sustenance and protection. He had learned early in his youth that they were far more concerned with the dead than they were with the living, and that included their son.

Stefan pushed the thoughts of self-reflection away and focused on the monitor. Vodka, as much as he enjoyed it, often caused his eye to turn inward and to examine his past.

He put the glass on the desktop, the alcohol splashing against the container.

Something had shown on one of the screens.

It was the camera that showed the street in front of the Commack house.

A dark blue sedan had pulled up and come to a stop. In the vehicle were two men. The driver appeared to be in his early forties. His passenger was much older.

Stefan watched them, gripping his knees with his hands and waiting to see what they would do. The two men spoke to one another, their words unheard. After several minutes, they exited the vehicle, the older man leaning on a cane. The driver came around the front of the car to stand with the passenger, and they stepped up onto the sidewalk.

For another minute, they stared at the house.

Then together they went up the short walkway and climbed the stairs to the front door.

Stefan breathed quickly through his nose, eager to see what the two would do next.

Chapter 48: At the House in Long Island

"I do believe this is a trap," Jeremy said.

Victor nodded his agreement. He had read the note tacked to the front door and had come to the same conclusion. The entire building had an uncomfortable air about it, and it made the hairs on the back of his neck stand up. His mouth was dry, and he felt as though he was about to walk blindly down a dark alley in which he had seen several unsavory individuals go before him.

"You don't have to do this, Victor," Jeremy said in a soft voice without looking at him. "You can wait out here. I will go in and let you know if it is safe to do so."

Victor shook his head. "No. No, I have to."

"Alright," Jeremy said. From the back seat of the car, he removed two small bags. They were fashioned from a mesh of lead strands placed between two layers of leather. Salt had been laced between the leather as well, and the bags would serve as temporary storage for any item that might serve as an immediate threat to their safety.

On the flight from New Orleans to New York, Jeremy had given an in depth explanation about the properties of certain items to help stop the dead. He had spoken of iron and salt, and how both the metal and the mineral could be used separately or in conjunction to stop and contain the dead. Jeremy had also explained the significance of lead and, depending on the ghost, the effects of religious items.

While Victor's education had been brief and concise, it had been extremely informative.

Jeremy passed one of the bags to Victor, then he took a pair of white gloves out of his pocket and handed them over as well.

Victor nodded his thanks and put them on, wincing as he slid one over his damaged, frost bitten hand.

"Will you be effective with your injury?" Jeremy asked as he put on his own gloves.

"That depends," Victor answered.

"On what?" Jeremy asked, glancing at him.

"Whether or not you'll be okay in there with a cane," Victor said, grinning.

Jeremy chuckled and gave a short bow. "Well said, my friend. Well said indeed. Now, let us enter this house and see what awaits us."

Victor could only nod. His throat had gone dry, and his tongue seemed to have swollen in his mouth. Images of the doll and the bear, the corpse of Mrs. Ducharme and Sue, when she had been possessed, all flashed through his mind.

If the house in front of them did belong to the person who had set the objects loose onto the world, then there was bound to be trouble beyond the door.

And Victor had no idea what that trouble might be.

Jeremy reached out, grasped the handle and opened the door.

A foul, rotten stench eased out of the house, rolling over them and spreading into the air. It was a noxious wave that stung Victor's eyes and caused him to gag.

"Never a good sign," Jeremy murmured.

"Damn, is there a body in there?" Victor asked, trying not to vomit.

"A body would be the least of our concerns," Jeremy said, stepping over the threshold.

Victor followed him, the floor creaking beneath their feet.

A glance around showed they were in a family room. There was a couch and a pair of recliners. An older, box shaped television stood on a worn table against the far wall. Pictures of family members hung in cheap gold frames on the walls and blinds were drawn against the rest of the world.

Victor stepped away from Jeremy and looked around, searching for some sign of the owner.

"Will you get the light please?" Jeremy asked.

"Sure," Victor replied, going to an end table and turning on a small lamp. A dull light spilled out from beneath its tattered, ivory shade. Three cherubs, carved from stone, clung to the center of the light, their feet planted on the base. Their heads were raised, staring up at the shaded bulb.

"Is that all there is?" Jeremy inquired, glancing over at the light. His eyes widened, and he hissed, "Step away."

Without asking why, Victor did as he was told. When he had reached Jeremy, he said, "What happened?"

"Nothing yet," Jeremy answered, his eyes fixed on the lamp.

"Is something supposed to?" Victor asked.

"Look," Jeremy replied, nodding back towards the light.

Victor turned around and bit back a gasp of surprise.

A trio of toddlers climbed out of the cherubs, the three ghost children squatting in predatory positions, their gaze locked on Victor and Jeremy.

"They can't do that," Victor said, not believing what his eyes were telling him.

"They can, and they do," Jeremy said. "We cannot take our eyes off them, Victor. One of us must be watching them at all times until we leave this room, and then we must be certain to close and lock the door."

"Who are they?" Victor asked.

"Later," Jeremy said, shaking his head. "Keep your eyes on them while I scout the next room."

"Sure," Victor said, his heart pounding.

Jeremy left him, and a moment later, there was a crash, and the older man cried out.

"Oh God, no!"

Before Victor could ask what happened a heavy weight smashed into the back of his chest and sent him into the floor.

And he lost sight of the children.

Chapter 49: The Fight Begins

Tin soldiers scattered across the old tile of the kitchen floor, the metal thumping and scraping, the troops skidding into dark corners and beneath the cabinets.

For the first time in years, Jeremy knew fear.

The temperature plummeted, and the first of the soldiers appeared.

He was a thin man, an officer, with a handlebar mustache. On his left eye, he wore a monocle. His right hand held a cavalry saber. He grinned at Jeremy and said, "Surrender, and you will be spared."

Jeremy knew that no answer he gave the man would stop what was about to come.

The officer repeated the statement, and when Jeremy still didn't reply, the soldier shrugged and shouted, "Attention!"

Four more ghosts appeared. They carried muskets with disturbingly long bayonets attached to them, and the soldiers leveled the weapons against him.

The officer raised his saber and spoke again. Each of the soldiers cocked their muskets, and Jeremy lifted his cane in salute.

A cunning smile appeared on the officer's face, and he snapped out an order.

The muskets were lowered, but the mustached man kept his saber high.

"A duel," Jeremy said.

The officer nodded, gave a short bow, and lunged towards Jeremy. As Jeremy went to block the attack, the officer reversed the blow and cut him across the back of his left arm.

The pain was instant and searing and had Jeremy been holding the cane in that hand, he would have dropped it.

A chuckle slipped out of the officer, and then he dashed forward, the saber point deadly in spite of its incorporeal nature.

Gritting his teeth, Jeremy slid a half step to the right, allowed the blade to pass through the bicep of his left arm, and bit back a howl as he swung his cane in towards the officer.

The iron filled handle caught the laughing ghost squarely on the side of the head, and the man vanished. Jeremy stumbled back, saw the looks of surprise on the faces of the remaining soldiers, and let out a pleased snort.

His joy was short lived as the ghosts charged at him, bayonets lowered.

A blow landed against his back, knocking him to the floor and Victor leaped over him. The younger man let out a cry of pain as one of the bayonets caught him in the thigh. Victor barreled through the man and crashed into the cabinets.

"Victor," Jeremy gasped, "there are toy soldiers on the floor, gather them up, and secure them!"

The other man nodded and spat out a single word through clenched teeth.

"Kids."

Jeremy had enough time to turn and see them crawling across the floor towards him, eyes wide and teeth bared.

Behind him, he heard Victor yell, but he couldn't spare the man a glance. The dead children would be on him, and they would do more than seek to feed on his flesh. They would rip out his soul if they could, and feast on it for as long as possible.

The toddlers were small, with chubby cheeks and limbs. But their eyes lacked any trace of innocence, and they had full sets of teeth. Each had been sharpened to a point, and Jeremy could only imagine the horrific pain as they bit into flesh.

Behind them the lamp remained lit, the stone forms they had abandoned once more looking up at the bulb.

"We know you, Jeremy Rhinehart," one of the dead children said. "We remember you. You sought to imprison us, to keep us away from food. That was not polite. You were not polite. I am afraid you lack manners."

Jeremy reached out for his cane and found it as the first of the toddlers found his foot. The teeth passed easily through the leather of his shoe, and the pain was as horrific as he had imagined it would be.

Chapter 50: The Soldiers

Victor jerked the bag open, grabbed the first tin soldier he saw and thrust it into the pouch. He cinched it shut as pain pierced his calf.

A scream tore out of his throat, and he twisted around to see one of the soldiers withdrawing a bayonet.

Victor's eyes darted around the kitchen, spotted a second soldier, and he threw himself across the floor at it. No sooner had he stuffed it into the bag with the first did another bayonet punch his shoulder. For a split second, he felt himself pinned to the floor, then the weapon was removed, and Victor spat at the soldier.

Three of them formed a semi-circle around him as he pushed himself upright, back against a cabinet. He spotted two of the soldiers, then the final one, all by the refrigerator.

The men glared at him, and he returned the expression and the sentiment. His eyes darted over their uniforms, taking in the cut of the jackets, the muskets and the hats they wore.

They were British, he realized. Late eighteenth century.

His mind raced as he sought out what he knew about the militaries of England at that time. From the deep recesses of his memory, he dragged up the basic concepts and formalities of King George's army.

One of the soldiers stepped forward, bayonet at the ready, and fear brought the language back to Victor.

"Attention!" he barked.

The three men snapped to the position of attention, and they looked at Victor with barely masked surprise.

Victor struggled to his feet and dragged up fragments of treatises on British military discipline.

"You dare to touch me?" he spat, the words coming out with difficulty.

Fear flickered over their faces.

Penalties in eighteenth-century armies had been brutal at best, and Victor recalled a project he had done about corporal punishment.

"It will be the wheel," he said, nodding as he took a painful step towards them.

One of the men started to shake, terror in all of their eyes.

"Move," Victor hissed, and the men moved as he stepped towards them. He bent down in front of the refrigerator, snatched up the toy soldiers, and turned to face the ghosts.

"Later," he said. With a shrug, he opened the sack and dropped the toy soldiers in. As he cinched it closed, the dead vanished. Victor turned to Jeremy and choked on a scream.

The toddlers had come into the kitchen.

Two of the three were latched onto Jeremy's feet while the older man fended off the third one, who was attempting to bite his face.

For a heartbeat, Victor stood still, unsure of what to do. Then he saw Jeremy's cane on the kitchen floor, and he leaped forward, snatched it up and swung it one-handed.

The handle passed through the child, the iron causing the ghost to dissipate.

Instantly, the other two abandoned Jeremy's feet and charged towards Victor, high-pitched squeals ripping out of their mouths.

Victor knocked them both back with the cane, the dead vanishing.

"They'll be back in moments," Jeremy gasped. "Go into the family room, unscrew the top of the cane. There is salt in it. Pour it out and make a circle. Put the lamp within the circle. Quickly now."

Victor didn't waste breath on an answer. Instead, he stumbled out of the kitchen, his body a massive ball of nerves and pain. The dead children appeared as he moved towards the lamp and he knocked them back again with the cane.

Hissing with pain, Victor forced his injured hand to unscrew the cane's handle. The strong smell of salt rose up from the confines, and he poured the contents out on the floor, making a rough, unbroken circle. He limped to the lamp, ripped it off the table and the plug out of the socket, and put both in the center of the salt ring.

Then Victor stepped back, screwed the handle back onto the body of the cane, and waited.

Nothing happened.

He glanced at Jeremy in the kitchen. The older man's face was a twisted mask of agony, but he had managed to sit up.

Victor took a step toward him, but Jeremy held up a hand, stopping him.

"No," Jeremy said, wincing. "Don't come any closer. I'm not sure what is a trap and what is not. The entire house could be, for all I know."

Victor glanced around, wary of every object, wondering if even the television was possessed.

"How are we going to get out of here?" Victor asked finally.

"That, my friend," Jeremy said with a forced smile, "is an excellent question. I am hopeful that in a moment I shall be able to get to my feet. When that is the case, I will endeavor to leave the kitchen."

"And then?" Victor asked.

"I will do what I should have done before I walked so blithely into the house," Jeremy said in a voice filled with bitter self-reproach. "I will look and see what needs to be seen."

"What are you talking about?" Victor asked, confusion mingling with the pain and causing a headache to burst into existence behind his eyes.

"If we make it out of this house," Jeremy said, his tone serious, "then I will tell you what I mean. Suffice to say I was foolish, and I do not plan to be so again."

As Victor watched, Jeremy got to his feet, staggered back and reached out. His hand found the lip of the countertop, slipped and struck a ceramic mug with a large letter 'E' emblazoned upon the side of it.

A shock wave of cold air rushed out of the kitchen, knocking Victor back a step and he heard Jeremy speak.

"Oh no," the man said in a soft voice, "it seems I've been foolish again."

Victor couldn't answer.

Something came roaring out of the kitchen.

***

Stefan watched the mug fall, the look of horror appearing at almost the same time on the old man's face.

He knows what it is, Stefan thought, grinning. *He knows who is coming.*

Chuckling, Stefan leaned back in his chair, crossed his arms over his chest, and waited to see what would happen.

Chapter 51: A Familiarity with the Dead

The house became darker as if a giant tarp had been dropped around it, cutting the building off from the rest of the world.

It was a disquieting feeling, and one Victor hoped would end sooner rather than later.

The house grew silent, and darkness filled the kitchen, blocking Jeremy from view.

Victor glanced down, made sure he wouldn't break the circle of salt and stepped away from the kitchen.

"Where are you going?" a voice asked.

It had a hollow ring to it, as though the words were spoken from a great distance.

"Evidently," Victor said, clearing his throat, "I'm not going anywhere."

The unseen ghost chuckled. "You're not stupid. I'll give you that. Although I don't know why you came in here. Didn't you know it was a trap?"

Victor started to answer and then stopped. The question, he realized, was rhetorical.

"Now," the ghost said, the voice taking on more definition, becoming masculine. "Tell me, what do you think I should do with you?"

"Let us go?" Victor suggested.

The ghost laughed and said, "No. Not likely. My name is Nicholas, and I have every intention of seeing if I can pull your intestines out through your mouth."

"Wow," Victor said in a small voice, "that does not sound like a good time at all."

"No?" Nicholas asked. "Hm, I suppose we're going to have to find out."

The darkness took shape, revealing a tall, thin man, his head nearly touching the lintel of the kitchen's doorway. His features were blurred as if he couldn't quite recall what he had looked like in life.

"Tell me," the ghost said, "what is your name? I should like to know it so when I question you there is a familiarity between us. So when I'm removing your ears, I might ask, how is this? And thus insert your name. I should not want us to be so impersonal. Death, my good, fine sir, should always be a personal business."

"Victor," he whispered, "my name is Victor."

"Victor," Nicholas said with satisfaction. "That is an uncommon name. I lived a great many years, you know, and only once did I know a Victor. He was named after my own father. A time when sons still respected their elders."

"Was he a good man?" Victor asked, desperate to stall his torture at Nicholas's hands.

"I don't know," Nicholas answered. "I died when he was still a babe in his mother's arms. It was that miserable cold New England weather that did me in. I am sure of it. You sound as if you are from that miserable portion of the States."

"I am," Victor said. "Pepperell."

Nicholas took a step forward and then stopped.

"Pepperell, did you say?" the ghost asked, his voice suddenly suspicious.

"Yes," Victor said, nodding. "I was born and raised there."

"What is your father's name?" Nicholas demanded, his voice rising.

"Alexander," Victor said hurriedly. "His name was Alexander."

"Was it?" Nicholas asked in a doubtful tone.

"Of course it was," Victor snapped, anger rising in spite of his fear, "I think I know the name of my father."

"And his last name, what is it?" the ghost asked softly.

"It was Daniels, just like mine is," Victor answered.

"Why do you speak of him in the past tense?" Nicholas asked.

"He's dead," Victor replied, fighting back the sadness that always accompanied thoughts of his father.

"No," Nicholas said, his voice rising. "You lie."

As Victor watched the ghost straighten up to his full height, easily six and a half feet.

"You lie!" the dead man bellowed. "My son is not dead!"

Victor couldn't move, his thoughts a mad whirlwind in the confines of his skull.

"He is not dead!" Nicholas screamed and the windows in the house shattered. From the kitchen, Jeremy howled, and Victor was driven to his knees. In his peripheral vision, he saw the grains of salt scattered.

The toddlers appeared instantly, converging on him.

"Did I say you could touch him?" Nicholas howled, striding forward. "Did I say you could touch my grandson?"

The dead children froze, their small eyes fixed on the tall, thin ghost.

"I did not," Nicholas hissed, swinging a large hand like a scythe. It cut through the three small ghosts as if they were nothing, and they vanished.

Victor sat down hard, staring at the ghost who towered over him. As he watched, the dead man's features solidified and took on definition. He saw a face he recognized from family pictures. Before him stood a familial figure of legend, a man of horrific temper and unquenchable rage.

Someone who had killed for the sheer pleasure of it.

Nicholas Daniels squatted down in front of Victor, waves of cold emanating from him. Soft gray eyes looked at him from deep sockets, and a genuine smile of joy cracked the man's hard features.

"A little grandson," Nicholas murmured, "And what bad company you have learned to keep."

Victor had no response. He could not see Jeremy, nor did he hear anything from the man. Nicholas occupied the whole of Victor's attention.

"Tell me, Victor," Nicholas said, shifting his weight from one foot to the next, "why are you here."

In short, stuttering sentences, Victor told his grandfather about the murder of Erin and the toys set loose in the world.

Collecting Death

Chapter 52: Words of Wisdom from Ivan Denisovich Korzh

After the cameras had gone black, Stefan turned off the monitor and stood up. He was disappointed that the equipment had died, but he had expected it as well, especially with Nicholas. The ghost was strong. Exceptionally so. It had come as no surprise then when he had drained the entire structure of the Long Island home of its electricity. Stefan chuckled as he thought of the electrical repairman that would more than likely discover the bodies of the two intruders.

With a yawn, Stefan stood up, stretched, and made his way out of the office. He wandered around the house for a few minutes, listening to the dead complain about their lot, and then made his way to the second floor. When he reached the top of the stairs, his father called to him, and Stefan rolled his eyes.

But he dutifully went to the barred and sealed door and announced his presence.

"You set a trap for them, didn't you?" his father asked in a low, dangerous voice.

"I did," Stefan said, fighting back the unease he felt at the tone in his father's voice.

"Did they arrive, Stefanushka?" his father whispered. "Did they fall into your little trap?"

"Arrived and were taken care of," Stefan said proudly, ignoring the sting of his father's tone.

"How do you have confirmation of this?" his father demanded. "Did you observe it in person?"

Stefan quickly explained what had occurred and his father asked, "Which of your mother's dead finished them off?"

"I don't know his name," Stefan confessed.

"What is he bound to?" Ivan asked, his voice revealing his impatience.

"A coffee mug," Stefan answered. "It has a large letter 'E' on it."

Silence greeted the statement.

Stefan waited for another few breaths, shrugged, and turned to walk away when his father spoke again.

"A letter 'E,'" Ivan Denisovich said, a curious note to his voice. "Tell me, Stefan Ivanovich, what did this ghost look like when he came out?"

Stefan frowned and answered, "Tall and thin. Almost like a scarecrow. I couldn't make out his face though. The cameras went out."

"Tall and thin," his father murmured, "and you let him out."

"I did," Stefan said. "I'll keep an eye on the news over the next few days."

The rest of his words were cut off as a blow passed through the door and launched Stefan back ten feet, tearing the breath out of his lungs.

"Fool!" his father screamed. "Stupid fool! You should have been stillborn! Do you know whom you have set free? Nicholas Daniels. He hunted men like us, Stefan. His collection was like nothing you have dreamt of. He slew us where we slept. Murdered our families and stole that which we had gathered. When he died, it was with that mug in his hands, so the story went, and he had bound himself to it so he could continue the hunt. Where was this mug you so casually employed for such a trifling matter?"

"Mom had it in her safe," Stefan said, his head spinning.

"And you didn't think that perhaps it was there for a good reason?" his father demanded. "You did not think to ask me about it?"

Stefan didn't know how to answer because his father would know the lie.

"Does he know where he was kept?" His father's voice was bitter when he asked the question.

"No," Stefan answered. "Not at all. We never spoke."

"Thank God for that, you imbecile," his father spat. "Is this house protected still?"

"Yes," Stefan confirmed.

"Good," his father grumbled, "you may not be able to leave for some time if Nicholas manages to escape the house."

"Would he come here?" Stefan asked uncomfortably.

"When he learns of it," Ivan answered, "you may rest assured that he will be here, and it is your head he will take.

And do not forget, my son, that I still expect you to retrieve your birthright."

Stefan remained silent, not only in regards to his father's expectations but about his feelings on his birthright, too.

Chapter 53: Unsure and Confused

Victor entered the Pepperell Police Station by himself, feeling a combination of guilt and paranoia. He knew that he had lied to the police about Sue, and he was worried that they did as well.

After the brutal fight in New York, he was still mentally drained. He expected an attack at any time, part of him certain that the entire phone call from the police had been nothing more than an elaborate ruse to bring him to the station. As the door clicked shut behind him, Victor expected a pair of burly officers to step out and place handcuffs around his wrists.

Yet nothing of the sort happened.

Instead, a young female receptionist looked up from her desk, smiled and asked, "May I help you?"

Victor nodded, swallowed, and said in a hoarse voice, "I received a phone call that I should stop by the police station when I got in."

The woman frowned, put a lock of brown hair back behind her ear and said, "May I have your name?"

Victor gave it to her and a look of pity flashed over the receptionist's face.

"Mr. Daniels," she said, "if you would wait here for a moment, Detective Eklund would like to speak to you about your home."

Victor nodded and stood in front of her desk, unsure as to what to do as she paged the detective. Less than a minute later, a dull gray steel door on the left opened and Detective Eklund stepped out.

He was a large man with a barrel chest and hands that looked as though they belonged to a professional boxer. The knuckles were cracked, red, and calloused. His beard was a dirty blonde and fell nearly to his chest while his head was shaved. He had a pair of thin reading glasses perched on the end of a nose that had been broken more than a few times and he extended a broad hand when he reached Victor.

Victor was surprised to find the detective's grasp firm but not crushing.

"I'm sorry to have to meet like this," Detective Eklund said, letting go of Victor's hand. "You've had a hell of a couple of weeks."

Victor thought that was a little too much of an understatement but he nodded in agreement.

"Now," the detective continued, "I'd like to ask you some questions if that's alright."

"Do we need to go into a room anywhere?" Victor asked, memories of television police dramas flickering through.

Detective Eklund shook his head. "No. Not at all. Do you know a Franklin Dipolito?"

"Um, no, I don't think so," Victor answered, confused. "Why?"

"Well, he may have had something to do with the fire," Detective Eklund said, "and while normally we wouldn't tell you that, I feel pretty confident in letting you know."

"Why's that?" Victor asked, his confusion deepening.

"Hm? Oh, well, he's dead," the detective said, sighing and shaking his head. "We found him inside of your house."

"Oh," Victor said softly, and he couldn't think of anything else to add.

"We were hoping that there was some sort of connection between the two of you," Detective Eklund continued. "Unfortunately, it seems like we won't be that lucky. Anyway, there are a few pieces of paperwork and such we need to go over with you, more for your benefit than ours. Insurance stuff. Could you follow me?"

"Um, sure," Victor replied and he followed the detective, his mind racing as he tried to think of where Rolf might be, and who he might possess next.

Chapter 54: Search and Destroy

Victor carried the lead-lined box in his hands, stepping over deadfall as he followed Jeremy, who was remarkably agile in spite of his cane.

"Are you sure about this?" Victor asked after several minutes of silence. Evening was settling over the landscape, and soon they wouldn't be able to travel any further without the assistance of flashlights.

"Of course I'm sure," Jeremy called over his shoulder. "From what the newspapers said, it was this family that was killed by Sue who was, as we know, possessed by Rolf. Franklin Dipolito lived across the street and, from what I've gathered, was arrested on multiple occasions for driving while intoxicated, making him a prime vessel for Rolf. I highly doubt that Rolf has gone anywhere without further assistance."

"But aren't we running the risk of being caught by someone?" Victor asked, shifting the box in his hands. "Someone has to be there, right? And why would he still be there?"

"Victor," Jeremy admonished, "Rolf needs a vessel first and foremost. Second, the man's ego is tremendous. Why should he fear either of us? Yes, he knows that we captured him once, but in the same breath he was out within a day. He will bide his time, as he has done so in the past."

Victor frowned and shook his head. "I don't know. I don't like it. I still think he's not going to be there, and that we'll end up being arrested for trespassing."

"No," Jeremy replied, "we won't be. I made some inquiries into the situation. It seems that the nearest family members live out in the mid-west and they won't be able to get here until sometime next week."

"How in God's name did you learn that?" Victor asked, surprised.

Jeremy chuckled. "I pretended to be a rather unsavory real estate agent and called up town hall. Now, rest assured, I am positive that Rolf is still within, and let us not forget, even your esteemed, dead grandfather confirmed my suspicions."

The sarcasm in Jeremy's voice with regards to Nicholas was unmistakable. Still, Victor asked, "Why didn't we ask him for help with capturing Rolf?"

The question caused Jeremy to stop and turn around. He had an incredulous expression on his face and he shook his head. "Victor, you are too smart to ask such a foolish question. Your grandfather was a brutal man. I knew of him, and of what he did. I would feel far more comfortable if you would allow me to lock him in a box and put him away. He is not to be trusted."

Victor didn't respond and his silence caused Jeremy to shake his head.

"Regardless," Jeremy continued, beginning to walk again, "he is right about where Rolf should be. I must warn you, though, it is more than likely going to be unpleasant."

Try burying your wife, Victor thought, but he didn't speak.

In a few minutes, the trees fell back and revealed a large backyard. An impressive house stood in front of them. All of the home's details were lost as Victor focused on the basement door.

"This is the house?" Victor asked.

Jeremy nodded.

An uncomfortable feeling settled in the pit of Victor's stomach as they crossed the yard, Jeremy's steps leading them unerringly to the basement door.

"What are you doing?" Victor asked, surprised.

"We have to go in," Jeremy stated, "he's in there, Victor. Waiting for us. Are you ready for him?"

Victor could only nod.

The door was unlocked, and it swung open on quiet hinges. From his pocket, Jeremy removed a small flashlight, turned it on, and stepped into the house. They moved in a few paces when the flashlight's beam illuminated Rolf, the bear sitting on the floor beside what Victor first thought was spilled paint, and then realized was dried blood.

"Get the box ready," Jeremy said, and the bear blinked.

The flashlight went dead and there was the rattle of metal. In the dim light of the evening seeping in through the open door, Victor caught sight of wrenches and sockets, nails and screws all flying towards them.

The effect was instant and painful, forcing him to clutch the lead box to his chest while wading through a storm of steel.

Jeremy went crashing down, yelling out in pain. Yet even as he did so, Victor saw the man's cane swing out, catch the bear and knock him toward Victor.

"Die!" Rolf screamed. A torrent of German followed and heavier items were ripped off the walls and torn from shelves. Something hard struck Victor in the side of the head and drove him to his knees. He lost his grip on the box and it fell to the floor. A hammer struck him in the chest, knocking the wind out of him and causing him to fall upon the box.

As items continued to smash against him, Victor managed to get his breath back as he pulled the box out from under him. With one hand, he opened it and with the other, he reached out, his fingers grazing the old, bitterly cold fur of the possessed toy.

A machine started up and it took him a moment to place the sound.

It was a generator.

As the machine began to thrum, the stench of exhaust crept into the air. The door to the basement slammed closed and Victor understood what the dead man wanted to do.

He was going to kill them with carbon monoxide.

Victor slapped his hand around, looking for something, anything heavy. His fingers grabbed hold of the hammer that had struck him and he twisted around with it, hurling it with all of his strength toward a window above a dry sink.

The tool smashed through the glass but even as the shards fell to the concrete floor, the exhaust thickened. A groan filled the air and Victor had only a fraction of a second to jerk out of the way of metal shelf that was torn from the wall.

Above the sound of the generator, Rolf's maniacal screaming could still be heard. In the dim light that filtered in through the broken window, Victor couldn't see the man. It was as though the old man had vanished.

Or that Rolf had ripped him out of the fabric of the universe and thrown him into some dark place.

A large wrench hurtled from the depths of a shadow and struck a brutally hard blow against the side of Victor's head.

Stars exploded as Victor fell down again, his head bouncing off the floor and causing him to howl in agony.

"Victor!" Jeremy yelled. "The box, Victor, the box!"

Pushing the pain aside, Victor twisted around, spotted the lead box and Jeremy.

The older man was close to the bear but the box was not.

Grinding his teeth against the pain, Victor scrambled forward on his stomach and grabbed hold of the lead box. He slid it across the floor to Jeremy.

The older man let out a fierce, triumphant shout and reached out a gloved hand, snatching up the bear.

Rolf's scream of rage and hatred punched through Victor's head and he collapsed to one side, vomiting.

Jeremy did not fare much better, and Victor saw the older man get sick as well. Yet in spite of his physical reaction to the dead man's scream, Jeremy pressed on. As if fighting against a gale force wind, Jeremy dragged the bear towards the open box.

Rolf's scream became a high-pitched shriek, and in the fading light, Victor watched as Jeremy thrust the bear into the box and slammed the lid down.

Items in flight plummeted to the floor, some of them landing on the two men.

In the sudden silence, Victor closed his eyes, not caring that he lay in a puddle of his own vomit. He pushed himself to his hands and knees and looked over at Jeremy.

"Come on, Victor," Jeremy said, coughing and picking up the box. "We need to get out of the house. The fumes."

Victor glanced at the generator, nodded and got to his feet. For a moment, he paused, coughing.

I'm alive, he thought, stumbling towards the door.

Alive.

And the creature that had killed Erin was captured.

Chapter 55: An Uncomfortable Bargain

Jeremy sat in the hotel room with Victor.

The battle in the house on Long Island had been four days prior, the battle to seize Rolf had occurred the night before, and he felt miserable. There was no permanent damage from what he could see, but once he was back in Norwich, Connecticut, he would see his doctor and make certain his amateur assessment was correct.

The two men were in a small hotel in Nashua, New Hampshire, several miles from the burnt remains of Victor's house. Slightly beyond his former residence was the Pepperell Police Station.

And now Rolf was in a lead box, the box itself on the center of the hotel room's table. Besides, it was a pale ceramic mug with a large letter 'E' upon it. And next to that was a bottle of cheap bourbon.

"I don't like it," Jeremy said, repeating the statement for the twentieth time.

"I know you don't," Victor replied. There was no sense of frustration in the answer. "You don't have to. Erin wasn't your wife. She wasn't your best friend."

Jeremy nodded even as he said, "I can keep him in the museum. He will be contained. We can't know what will happen when the bear is destroyed."

"The bear won't be destroyed," Nicholas said, appearing in the room and filling it with darkness. "I don't believe you understand that, Mr. Rhinehart."

Jeremy shivered at the sound of his name spoken by Nicholas. He knew of the man's history, of the violence he had wreaked upon the world.

The man had been a butcher and Jeremy doubted that that had changed with death.

"Can we be sure though?" Jeremy asked, pressing the issue.

"I have been many things in my time, Mr. Rhinehart," Nicholas said, chuckling, "but a liar was never one of them. Leave me to my task. It is easy enough for me."

Jeremy shook his head but said nothing more.

Nicholas turned to Victor and said, "Now, grandson, drink, and drink well. The quicker you are drunk, the quicker this can end for you."

"It won't end here," Victor said in a low growl. "It will end when I find the person who sold the damned bear to Erin."

Nicholas chuckled. "Yes, you are my grandson. We will do wonders together, Victor. Absolute miracles. Now drink."

Jeremy watched as Victor reached out, took hold of the bottle and twisted the metal cap off. He dropped it to the table, where it clinked, and raised the bottle to his lips. Jeremy closed his eyes and shook his head.

The smell of bourbon filled the room as did the dead man's laughter.

***

Rolf felt the tight bonds of lead relax, and he surged out of the confines of the bear.

He found himself in a small room, standing beside a bed. Rhinehart sat at a table, Victor beside him. A half-empty bottle of liquor stood beside a coffee mug, and the box that had so recently kept him prisoner.

Rolf nearly shouted with joy as he realized that Victor was drunk.

He took a step forward to claim the man's flesh as his own when Victor's head turned towards him, the eyes wide and gray.

Rolf hesitated.

He glanced around, the room felt strange to him, as though it wasn't all that it seemed. With a cautious eye on Victor, Rolf tried to slip through the wall.

He couldn't.

"Where are you going, Rolf?" Victor asked, and while the voice was his, the inflection was off.

With a growing sense of fear, Rolf realized he wasn't speaking with Victor. In silence, he tried to push through the floor and couldn't.

Rolf was trapped. Snarling, he demanded, "Who are you?"

"Me?" the other asked. "You know me. But not like this. My name is Nicholas. Do you remember me?"

Rolf did.

He threw himself at the wall and bounced off it.

"Trying to leave?" Nicholas asked, standing up. He strode forward without any semblance of being drunk.

"What are you going to do?" Rolf hissed, shrinking back, knowing he couldn't fight the creature in front of him.

"Hm, an excellent question," Nicholas responded. "I don't think you are deserving of an answer though. Do you?"

Before Rolf could reply, Nicholas reached out and grabbed him by both arms.

Nicholas, with Victor's hands, was able to pin his arms to his side. It was a terrible, horrific feeling and he tried to pull his right arm free.

Which he did, in a way, for he left the arm in Victor's grasp.

"Yes," Nicholas murmured, "I believe this shall be the perfect way to dispose of you."

"No," Rolf begged, "please, you don't know what will happen."

"No," Nicholas replied, "I do not. You, however, will know soon enough."

He dropped Rolf's right arm to the floor, where it slowly faded from view. Casually, Nicholas reached up and yanked Rolf's ear off his head.

Rolf gasped and sobbed, tried to sink to his knees and felt himself jerked up once more.

"My grandson told me," Nicholas said in a low, calm whisper, "that you murdered his wife. I find this especially egregious, and I do believe that you're no longer welcome here."

Rolf felt his other arm being torn away and he screamed, a long, painful sound that caused Nicholas to let out a thrilled laugh.

Chapter 56: Preparations for the Hunt

Victor's head felt as though a thousand hammers were landing blows upon it. Groaning, he picked up his water, took another pair of aspirin and washed them down.

"Still not better?" Jeremy asked.

"No," Victor answered. "Cheap bourbon."

"Cheap bourbon and possession," Jeremy corrected his voice carrying a note of sadness in it.

Victor wanted to feel bad about disappointing the man the night before, but he couldn't. Nicholas had offered vengeance and had provided it. The bear Rolf had possessed was once more only an antique toy. Jeremy would bring it down to Connecticut and keep it secured in his museum.

"Will you really keep Nicholas with you?" Jeremy asked.

"Yes," Victor answered. "I have to. He'll help us find the seller."

"Do you believe that?" Jeremy asked.

Victor nodded and instantly regretted the act. Groaning, he answered, "Yes. I do."

"And what does he ask of you in return?" Jeremy's voice was soft.

Victor coughed uncomfortably and replied, "That he gets use of my body once in a while."

"You find this acceptable?" Jeremy asked.

"To kill whoever killed Erin?" Victor asked. "You're damned right I do."

"It is a deal with the devil, you've struck," Jeremy warned. "There is no easy way off this path once you have started."

"I figured as much," Victor said.

After a moment of silence, Jeremy said, "I'm going to bring the bear to my house and put it away. Then I'm going to make a list of the items that I know the Korzhs had. If you want to start researching their child, then I am hopeful we will each have some actionable information when we meet again in a week or so."

"You're going to help me?" Victor asked in surprise.

"I won't help you take your vengeance," Jeremy corrected, "but I will help you track the seller down. No more of these items can be let loose on the world."

"I know," Victor agreed.

"Well then," Jeremy said, getting to his feet, "I will speak with you in a day or two. Earlier if something of significance jumps out at me."

"Alright," Victor said. He waved good-bye as Jeremy let himself out of the hotel room. Less than a heartbeat later the room darkened.

"You know what I have not done in a terribly long time, grandson?" Nicholas asked.

"No," Victor said, wincing while turning to look at his dead grandfather.

The man stood by the bathroom as he said, "I have not eaten a steak. An honest to God, American steak."

"Well," Victor said, "let's see what we can do about that."

And with a grimace, he picked up the half-empty bottle of bourbon from the table and started to drink.

Chapter 57: The Cemetery

The cemetery was old, with some of the headstones dating back to when Pepperell had been founded in 1775. Tall trees lined the fieldstone wall and cast dappled shadows on the gathered dead. The sod had yet to take over Erin's grave and the edges of it were yellowing.

I'll have to bring water next time, Victor thought.

He sat down on the grass, wrapped his arms around his knees, and stared at the place where Erin's own headstone would be. The flowers had been removed, per the regulations of the cemetery, and Victor didn't mind. Seeing them wilting above his wife's grave would have been another reminder of how alone he was.

Alone and without any of the mementos of their life together.

Rolf had robbed him not only of his wife but also of their physical history.

No photographs of their wedding existed. None of the presents they had exchanged. Not their favorite movies or their beloved books. Her childhood dolls and his Star Wars action figures.

Everything was gone.

Every piece of their life had been erased and at some point, Victor knew, he too would begin to forget.

And there would be nothing to help him remember.

Rolf had been the thief of dreams. The murderer.

But he had been taken care of. Nicholas had seen to that, tearing the ghost to shreds according to what Jeremy had said.

At the thought of the older man who had helped Victor so much in regards to Rolf, Victor closed his eyes and dropped his head onto his knees. For several minutes, he stayed in that position, listening to the birds and the squirrels in the trees.

Jeremy had asked Victor to accompany him on the quest to find the seller, the one who had shipped Rolf to Erin. The unknown individual had sent out others, and they too had caused damage, but Victor didn't care about them.

He only cared about Erin.

She was all he had ever cared about.

Victor lifted his head up and stared at the dull outline around her grave.

"I'm going to go for a bit," Victor whispered. "I'll come back. I need to find who did this to us. I love you, Erin."

His eyes stung but no tears fell.

He was too angry to weep.

Victor got to his feet, looked down and said, "I'll be back. I promise."

He turned to leave and the wind blew, sounding as if someone asked him a single question.

When?

"When I put them in the ground," Victor answered, and he left the cemetery in silence.

Chapter 58: Done Alone

"Tell me when you are going to return!" his father snapped.

"I can't because I'm not sure," Stefan answered, struggling with the feelings of guilt swirling in him.

"Where are you going?" Ivan demanded.

"It's better if I don't tell you, Father," Stefan replied, wincing.

His father's anger pulsed into the room.

"I do not like this," his father stated in a dull, flat voice. Stefan fought the urge to run for the front door.

"I have to move the collection," Stefan explained again. "If I don't, I might lose it to that pair of undeserving men."

"You're lying," his father snarled. "And you still refuse to retrieve that which you have sent out. You are destroying your birthright!"

Kind of the point, Stefan thought, but didn't say as much to his father. He struggled with the feeling of hate and fear warring within him. "I can't explain it now."

"No," his father hissed, cutting him off, "you won't explain it now. There is a difference, Stefanushka, and you are stepping around it. There is something you need to remember."

"What's that?" Stefan asked, eager to leave before his father's temper became too hot.

"I can always find out what you are doing, my son," Ivan said in a low voice. "These walls may contain the others, but they will not contain me. There are those that will help Ivan Denisovich Korzh if he calls to them."

"Okay," Stefan said, worry and fear crawling around his stomach, "well, I've got a lot of driving to do. I'll be back as soon as I can."

"See that you are," his father said, and went silent.

Stefan hurried out of the house, locking it behind him. He would return, after he was settled in Kansas. The state was big, and he would be able to continue with his work of killing the amateurs. And when that was done, he would move on to the older ones.

The bad ones.

Stefan went to the RV he had purchased, climbed into it and glanced around. The dead were silent, secured in boxes and containers stacked around the vehicle. He had hours to go before he would rest. For a moment, he considered the setback he had suffered with the loss of the house in Long Island, and the items that had been in it, but then he smiled.

Soon he would be in his new home, and none would be the wiser.

Whistling, Stefan started the RV, shifted into gear, and pulled out of the driveway. Life, once more, was looking up.

* * *

Bonus Scene

Bonus Scene Chapter 1: Stefan Korzh Hunts

A harsh wind ripped down the center stairwell of the apartment building, causing Stefan to huddle against the cold concrete wall. The white cotton gloves on his hands were too large and provided little protection from the chill. He pulled the small box closer to his chest and waited for the cold to pass.

It did so after nearly a minute, and when it had gone, he straightened up and continued towards the fifth floor. When he climbed past the third, his legs began to tire. Anger at his own physical weakness smothered his body's complaints, and he focused on each stair. The worn treads of steps were slick from decades of use, and he had to watch where he placed each foot. His sneakers weren't new, and what little grip was left on the soles might not prove to be enough for the ascent.

Stefan reached the landing for the fourth floor and paused, taking a moment to make certain no one was following him.

He was alone on the stairs, as he had thought he would be. Most people would take the elevators. And Stefan knew that no one would notice him, a thirteen-year old boy, in a structure as large as Crisp, Building 1.

And Stefan had been careful.

He had chosen the Crisp apartments, and he watched them. In the weeks prior to the adventure, he had found his mark there and made certain he knew everything about her habits.

Stefan waited a full minute to make certain he was alone, and then continued his ascent. Soon he reached the fifth landing, but he hesitated at the door that led to the floor. The day prior, he had slipped a wedge made of folded paper into the lock to stop it from catching. With a gloved hand, he reached out, took hold of the worn metal door latch and tugged on it gently.

The door slid on silent hinges, the smell of the WD-40 he previously used still strong in the air.

He edged the door a fraction of an inch past the frame and peered into the hall beyond. The hall was empty, as he had hoped it would be.

Stefan pulled the door open far enough for him to slip in, and then eased it closed behind him. The sounds of televisions and people arguing reached his ears. A horrific wave of mixed aromas assaulted his nose, stinging his eyes and causing him to bite back a cough. He hated the smells of other people, and the food that others ate was the worst.

Stefan shook the distractions away and focused on his target instead.

Apartment 515, seven doors down on the right from where he stood.

There was a light green, faux grass mat with the word 'Welcome' spelled out in letters formed of sunflowers. Bright pictures of fairies and gardens, beautiful flowers and snow-capped mountains were taped to the metal door. A spider plant hung on either side of the door, and there was a sign to the right that said, "There are no strangers here, only friends we have not met."

Stefan hated all of it.

He crept closer, hesitating when passing each door, readying the excuses he had prepared.

Yet no one left the safety of their apartments to investigate the stranger on their floor.

No one cared.

When Stefan reached her door, he squatted down and pried open the lid of the wooden box. In its confines lay an origami rose, the open bud a vibrant, almost pulsing red. He extracted it with a care that bordered on reverence and laid it on the left side of the mat. She was left-handed, he knew, and it would be natural for her to glance there before she entered her home.

A chill filled the hall, rising up from the paper rose. The air pulsed in front of him and a shape began to form.

"Stop!" he hissed in Russian.

The shape fluctuated between definition and ambiguity.

"I will crush you," he whispered, "and then I will bring you to my father."

The form vanished.

Stefan nodded in approval. "A woman will come here soon enough. She is yours."

A low, dry chuckle escaped from the origami rose and Stefan stood up. Long strides carried him back to the door that led to the stairs. He pushed it open, removed the paper wedge and placed it in the back pocket of his jeans. With the door only slightly ajar, Stefan settled in and waited.

Time passed, and people came and went from the other apartments. None of them noticed the origami flower, and none of them went near the stairs. All made their way to the elevators at the end of the hall.

At 6:26 PM one of the elevator doors opened, and she came out.

Mrs. Anise, who helped run the library at school.

Her husband had been murdered, so the story went, and she had sought refuge in anonymity. She put the books away in the school library and made sure everyone behaved.

More than once she had sought to put a smile on Stefan's face by telling him jokes, or giving him a piece of candy.

But he didn't need sweets or amusement.

Stefan needed to be left alone. He had told her in no uncertain terms that she had to stop talking to him, but that had earned him a trip to the principal's office. The trip to the head of the school had resulted in a phone call home. He had received a whipping from his father, and a slap from his mother.

Then they had promptly ignored him again and returned to their pursuit of the dead. All Stefan had received for his honesty was punishment, so there would be no more discussions with Mrs. Anise about what he did or did not want or need.

The rose would solve the problem as well as satisfy his curiosity about one of the items in his mother's collection.

And so he settled in behind the door, kept his eye pressed to the slim crack, and waited for Mrs. Anise to come home.

Bonus Scene Chapter 2: A Rose is a Rose

When the elevator doors opened, the familiar smells of her floor washed over Eileen Anise. She smiled at them and the sounds that wrapped around her. From apartment 201 she heard Mr. Daly singing along to an Italian opera. Apartment 202 had the familiar noise of cartoons. The next pair of apartments were silent, their occupants still in the city. In 204 lived a man by the name of Hall and the rhythmic click and clack of a keyboard slipped out. Eileen had spoken to him a few times, and she had learned he was a writer, although he wouldn't tell her of what.

Humming to herself, Eileen walked at a slow, leisurely pace to her own apartment. When she arrived, she fished her keys out of her purse, went to unlock the door and paused.

On her welcome mat was a small, origami rose.

A smile spread across her face as she bent down and picked it up. The rose was delicate, the folds far more intricate than any other piece of origami art she had seen. Eileen straightened up, held the rose closer and wondered how anyone's hands could do such delicate, precise work.

And she wondered who would be so phenomenal as to leave such a piece of art on her doorstep.

Once more, a happy hum came unbidden to her lips, and she let herself into the apartment. Eileen paused to place the wedge beneath the door, propping it open as was her habit when she came home.

She always cooked a large dinner, as if her husband still would be coming home from a day at Public Works.

More often than not, she had company for her late evening meal. Usually the Pallis twins, whose mother was out doing unspeakable things to put food on the table and pay the bills. Eileen shuddered at the thought and went to the dining table. She set the rose down at her place and hung her purse up in the kitchen. Then, with a nod to herself, Eileen went about the business of fixing dinner.

Soon, water boiled on the stove for the pasta while ground beef browned in the stove. Red sauce, from a jar, since she didn't have the patience to make her own, simmered in a pan on the backburner.

Satisfied that the various ingredients would finish at the same time, Eileen went to the table, sat down, and picked up the rose.

The paper was smooth, feeling as though it had been made from silk. It was also cold to the touch, the sensation sharp and unpleasant.

But it was too beautiful to put down.

Eileen held it up closer so she could examine it without having to squint or dig her reading glasses out of her purse. She rotated the paper flower, her fingers becoming numb as she held it.

Then the rose moved.

At first, she thought it was her eyes, tired from cleaning the shelves at the library. A moment later, she was sure it was a trick of the light, or perhaps the flower unfolding from her handling of it.

But it was none of those.

Instead, the paper petals opened with a casual, elegant grace that snatched the breath from her mouth and left Eileen filled with wonder. She brought the flower even closer, her heartbeat increasing.

The unmistakable scent of a rose filled her nose, and she felt her eyes widen with wonder.

She closed her eyes, inhaled deeply, and then gagged as the powerful aroma transformed into a putrid stench. Gagging, Eileen dropped the origami flower.

Yet the paper clung to her fingers.

She shook her hand, but the flower wouldn't fall. Gritting her teeth, she shook her hand even harder, and let out a yelp of surprise and pain.

The rose petals had sprouted thorns, and each of the sharp barbs had sunk themselves into the tender flesh of her fingertips.

"Do you like my flower?" a voice asked from behind her.

Eileen spun in her chair with enough force to knock herself loose, falling to the floor and landing with a heavy, painful thud.

A short man stood behind her chair, his form not fully conceived. It seemed to fade in and out of existence as if someone was opening and closing a glass door. At times, he was nothing more than a murky image; at others he was completely visible.

Through the shock and pain, Eileen noticed that he wore battered overalls and had a face that was weathered from long years in the sun. Wrinkles rippled around his eyes and mouth. A large brimmed straw hat hid his eyes, and the fingers on his large hands were crooked and bent. His boots were large and scarred, covered with dirt that they would never be free from.

"Can't you speak?" the man asked, his head tilting to the left.

Numbed by the surreal events, Eileen could only nod.

"Then do so," the man commanded.

Eileen tried, stuttered, then let out a sharp cry of shock as the rose's thorns burrowed deeper into her.

"What do you want me to say?" she gasped.

The man frowned, shook his head and said, "That won't do. Not at all."

"What won't do?" Eileen asked, trying again to shake the rose off but only encouraging the bizarre origami to cling with greater tenacity.

"Your voice," the man explained, "it is not sweet. Which means you are not sweet. And since I must have fertile and flavorful soil for my rose, you are not it. She cannot live within you."

Eileen didn't know why, but she sobbed with relief at the man's statement.

That relief vanished with his next sentence.

"But you can feed her," the man said, and he nodded.

Before Eileen could do more than blink, the rose unfolded itself, again and again until the red paper could have covered Eileen twice over.

And it started to.

The paper wrapped around her ankles snaked up her calves and bound her knees together. She tried to kick free, but as she was occupied, the piece of the rose anchored in her hand jerked her arm to her side. Horrified, Eileen opened her mouth to scream, but the paper wrapped around her chin and the top of her head, cinching down tightly and snapping her teeth together.

She let out a terrified moan and toppled over, the paper constricting around her like a great snake. The ghost stood in the same spot, watching her.

Beyond him, Eileen saw a figure in the doorway, and she felt a desperate surge of hope.

She recognized the person, it was Stefan Korzh, the curious little boy who was always reading about ghosts in the school library.

But as her eyes locked with his, she noticed there was no sympathy to be seen. He watched her, his plain features unmarred by concern or excitement.

Eileen tried to call his name, but she gagged instead.

"Now it's time for her to eat," the man explained, "it may take some time though, and she's none too gentle about it either."

That, Eileen, realized as the paper tore a large chunk of her cheek away, was a terrible understatement.

Bonus Scene Chapter 3: At Home

"Where were you?" Stefan's mother asked as he walked down the stairs.

"Outside," Stefan answered.

His mother looked up from the catalog that had arrived in the mail earlier and frowned at him. "What were you doing outside?"

He smiled and answered, "I was looking at flowers."

Her brows furrowed with confusion. "You hate flowers."

"Most of them," he corrected. "Not all. What's for dinner?"

"Soup," she answered, turning her attention back to the catalog.

Stefan knew he was lucky to get even soup when a new list of items arrived. Still, he hated her for her lack of domesticity during those times. He could only hope it would be a small selection, one that wouldn't keep her occupied for too long. If it did, he would be eating soup for three meals a day until she was done.

"Your father called," she said as Stefan turned to go into the kitchen.

"Yes?" Stefan asked, hesitating in the doorway.

"He may be home tonight," his mother continued without a glance towards him. "He is nearby, bargaining with someone for a piece."

Then she straightened up, stretched and added, "Evidently, there is someone else who is seeking to purchase the piece."

Stefan faced his mother again. "That's not smart."

"No," she agreed, "it usually isn't. I don't want your father beating anyone up again. I don't want to waste any money on bailing him out."

Without responding, Stefan stored away the statement for later. Should his father find fault with him for some reason, then sharing his mother's thoughts would distract the man long enough for Stefan to find a safe hiding place.

Once in the kitchen, he rummaged around for a can of soup that could fulfill two basic requirements. The first was that the soup had not passed its expiration date. More than once he had found canned goods that were older than him in the pantry. And second, the soup would be one he could actually stomach, regardless of whether or not it was still good.

He found a can of pork and beans in a back corner and was surprised to see it had not yet expired. Grinning, Stefan went to the countertop, pulled out the can opener and then came to a stop. He listened and felt uncomfortable.

The house was silent.

His entire life had been filled with the noises of the dead, moaning and complaining from the objects they were bound to.

From the dining room came the screech of chair legs on the floor and his mother appeared a moment later, an expression of frantic worry on her face.

"What's going on?" she asked in a whisper. "Why are they all quiet?"

"Don't ask me," Stefan said, putting as much bluster and bravado as he could into his voice. "They're *your* pets."

Normally, the remark would have earned him a slap or even the confiscation of his food.

This time his mother didn't seem to hear him.

"What's going on?" she demanded, doing an admirable job of keeping the fear out of her voice.

None of the dead responded.

"Tell me!" she ordered.

A small child appeared by the back door. Stefan forgot her name, but he had seen her before. She had once owned a teapot.

"He used Horatio," the little girl said. And then she vanished.

"What do you mean?" his mother called out after her.

Stefan stiffened, grasped the can of food as tightly as he could, and took a small step back.

"What did she mean?" his mother asked, confused, glancing over at him. The confusion on her pale, puffy face vanished as she saw his expression.

"Stefan," she said, anger exploding out of his name, "what did she mean?"

"I don't know," Stefan lied, taking a larger step towards the hall. "What do any of them mean? They're all crazy."

"Tell me," his mother hissed, fury lighting her pale brown eyes. "Tell me what she meant, damn it!"

Without a word, he turned and raced for the hallway.

Instead of freedom and safety, he ran into the broad, muscled chest of his father.

The man's equally large hand swung back and crashed down, striking Stefan on the side of the head and smashing him into the wall. Stefan lost control of his limbs and slid face down to the worn runner on the floor. He tasted blood in his mouth, and an ache settled in his head even as he slipped into unconsciousness.

Bonus Scene Chapter 4: Punished and Unhappy

"What did you think you were doing?" his father demanded.

Stefan spoke slowly, his jaw aching. With each word formed he winced, but he managed to answer.

"I wanted to see what would happen," Stefan said. It was half of the truth, but at least there was truth in it. His father might suspect him of withholding information, but he wouldn't think he was lying.

The large man's face pockmarked and ravaged from some childhood disease, frowned.

"You wanted to see what would happen," his father muttered. "Perhaps I should ask who this person was that suffered to satisfy your curiosity?"

Stefan didn't respond.

"No," his father sighed, "I think not. Too much information in this situation might be worse than none at all."

Silence fell over them as Stefan kept his eyes away from his father's. Any sort of challenge to Ivan Denisovich Korzh came at a heavy price, and Stefan's body already ached from the single blow he had received earlier.

His father cracked the knuckles on each hand, leaned a thick shoulder against the frame of the doorway and stated, "You are not a stupid child. You chose Horatio with care, I am sure. A choice tailored to your victim."

Stefan kept his face free of any expression, and his father let out a grim chuckle.

"Yes," Ivan said, "I can see it perfectly. Someone thrilled with nature and art. A girl. Or perhaps a woman, someone who has slighted you in some way."

Stefan's heart began to race, and he felt the veins pulse beneath the skin. His face grew red, and the increase in blood flow caused the pain he felt to magnify.

"Yes," Ivan whispered, "that is it exactly. But it was no girl. No. You would have chosen something finer for a girl, and not merely some folded paper rose. This is a woman who has focused herself on art. And her crime, what was it?"

Stefan reined in his heartbeat with difficulty before he answered, "I don't know what you're talking about."

His father's laugh shook the bedroom walls, and Stefan was thankful that the man found humor in his denial.

"Keep your secret, Stefanushka," his father said, "but do not think you shall be let off easy for this offense. I shall discuss with your mother what sort of punishment would be fitting. I will have this from you though, you will not steal from your mother after this moment, is that understood?"

The last words were spoken in a harsh, low tone that Stefan had heard far too many times to take lightly.

In silence, he nodded his head.

"Good," his father said, and he left the room, closing the door behind him.

Stefan listened to the man's loud steps as they retreated down the hall, then thundered down the stairs. Soon his parents would discuss his punishment, and he had promised not to steal from his mother again.

Stefan lay back on his bed, flinching at the pain. He snaked a hand under his pillow, found the bolt and grabbed hold of it.

A weak smile, battered by the steady throb of his injuries, crept onto his face as he cupped the worn metal to his chest.

He hadn't lied to his father.

Stefan wouldn't steal from his mother again because he had already stolen what he needed. And soon he would use the bolt the same way he had used the origami flower.

From around the house, he heard the rise and fall of the complaints of the dead. Beneath those sounds came the familiar tune of his mother and father arguing. And it was to those noises Stefan drifted off, dreaming about what he would do as soon as fate allowed him to.

Bonus Scene

Bonus Scene Chapter 5: A Conversation in the Woods

Stefan found his freedom restricted.

His parents, in their infinite wisdom, no longer allowed him to go and play with his friends.

He felt it was a curious sort of punishment because he hadn't had any friends since he was nine years old. Then again, his parents had stopped paying attention to him around that time as well. The dead and the items they possessed had taken up what little had been available to Stefan.

So, his being required to remain in the backyard, and the woods behind it, which didn't affect him for either good or ill.

Stefan left the house, passed through the yard and entered the trees. The birds ceased their calls as he neared them, and squirrels seemed to flee his presence. Stefan fantasized that it was him they were afraid of, but he knew that wasn't the case. They were afraid of what he carried.

When he was far enough in so he could hear his father approach before the man might see him, Stefan found a comfortable place to sit down. After he had settled in, Stefan withdrew the bolt from his front pocket and held the worn metal up. It, like the origami rose, was cold to the touch, and it made him smile.

"Come out, come out," he said in a soft voice, and his ears popped painfully as if there had been a sudden change in air pressure.

A teenager, who looked only slightly older than Stefan, sat across from him. The other boy was gray and opaque. His features were long and narrow, his eyes placed too close together. A large bump interrupted the slope of his nose, and he licked at the corners of his mouth in a way that made Stefan wonder whether or not the other boy even knew that he was doing it.

"Who are you?" the new boy asked.

"Stefan," he answered, "who are you?"

The other boy hesitated, then said, "Erik. Erik Powers. Erik Powers, Senior."

"Your father's dead," Stefan said.

Erik nodded. He glanced around and said, "So am I. I didn't have no kids though. Ain't no juniors running around."

Stefan didn't respond to Erik's comment, and he kept his lack of interest in the matter to himself. He hadn't awakened the ghost to discuss matters of familial lineage.

"I need a favor from you," Stefan said, repeating what he had written down. He had memorized the small speech, tailoring it to the dead teenager in front of him.

Erik's small eyes narrowed and focused on him.

"What sort?" the ghost asked.

"The killing kind," Stefan answered.

Erik sniffed and looked away. "Don't know why you're talking to me about killing."

Stefan repressed a smile and asked, "No?"

Erik shook his head.

Stefan held up the bolt and cleared his throat.

Erik glanced at him, and his eyes widened in surprise.

"I was amazed," Stefan said, "at the damage, the lack of a single bolt could cause to a ship's engine."

"Don't know what you're talking about," Erik said, stuttering.

"Yes, you do," Stefan said, closing his fist around the bolt. "You were an able-bodied seaman on the USS Cyclops. She was lost in 1918. All hands missing. All except for you, you managed to slip away in Barbados when the ship stopped in for coal."

"He had it coming!" Erik hissed, his voice sinking to a low rasp. "Captain Worley was a miserable man. He didn't treat us any better than beasts!"

"I believe you," Stefan whispered, "but I need you to help me because you know about killing."

Erik looked uncomfortable for a moment, then he nodded reluctantly.

"Who?" he asked.

Stefan kept a serious expression on his face as he said, "At the end of this path is a house. In the yard, there's a man. I need you to kill him."

"Why?" Erik asked, glancing at the trail that led away from them.

"It doesn't matter," Stefan said, putting a note of command in his voice. "I need you to do it. That's all."

"Alright," Erik said, getting to his feet. "I'll do it."

The ghost moved along the path, leaving Stefan alone in the woods.

When he was sure that Erik was far enough away, Stefan allowed himself a little smile. Then, from his shirt pocket, he removed a small box the size of a deck of playing cards. But it was far heavier, the entirety of it made from lead.

Stefan lifted the lid, put the bolt in it and set it on the ground with the lid still open. While he waited for Erik's return, Stefan began to dig a small hole, just big enough for the box.

***

Fredrick Welsh picked the last of his squash and put it in the basket behind him. He straightened up, tried to ignore the arthritic pain in his back and hips and knees, and took a handkerchief out of his back pocket. Frederick shook out the blue cloth, wiped sweat from the back of his neck and off his forehead, and then returned the handkerchief to its place.

A cool breeze sprang up, and he shivered, looking up at the afternoon sky and the trees lining his yard.

There were no clouds to speak of, and the trees were still. Not a branch moved, nor did any of their leaves.

Confused, Frederick sought out the source of the breeze and instead found a teenager.

He was short and wiry, a slight hunch to his back and he wore torn and tattered clothes.

"Are you alright?" Frederick asked, concerned. "Do you need help?"

A look of misery flashed across the young man's face, but he shook his head, saying only, "I'm sorry."

"Why are you sorry?" Frederick asked, worry creeping up. He opened his mouth to speak again, but instead of words coming out, he vomited.

Salt water shot out past his lips and knocked his dentures free. His stomach clenched and he gasped for air, spewing the bitter liquid out. No matter how hard he tried to catch his breath, he couldn't.

He was drowning.

Frederick fell to his hands and knees, head hanging down as salt water exploded out of his mouth and nose. The force of his own vomiting drove him to the ground, causing him to knock over the basket of squash.

And over the sound of his own death, Frederick heard the young man apologizing again and again.

Bonus Scene

Bonus Scene Chapter 6: Lessons Learned

When Erik returned, he looked miserable.

"Is he dead?" Stefan asked.

Erik nodded and dropped down, sitting across from Stefan and not meeting his gaze.

"How?" Stefan inquired, keeping his excitement bottled up.

Erik told him, in halting sentences, how he had drowned the man. When he finished with the explanation, the dead sailor asked, "Why? Why did he have to die?"

"Hm?" Stefan said. "Oh, him? I wanted to know how you killed."

Erik looked at him with an expression of horror.

"He didn't do nothing wrong?!" Erik howled. "He was innocent!"

Stefan frowned. "I never worried about whether he was innocent or not. I never even thought about it. Who knows, really."

The dead sailor got to his feet, his face twisted with rage.

"You can't just go around murdering folk who ain't done nothing!" Erik screamed.

"Of course I can," Stefan retorted. "I can do whatever I want. Whenever I want. Well, so long as my father doesn't catch me."

"I won't let you," Erik said, sudden determination entering his voice. "You can't do stuff like that anymore. Not anymore."

The ghost took a step towards Stefan and said, "You'll drown too."

Stefan tasted saltwater in his mouth, reached out and slapped the lid closed on the box.

Erik vanished, and Stefan spat a mouthful of the foul water out onto the forest grounds.

Stefan smiled to himself and covered the lead box up with the dirt he had extracted. Once it was buried, he got to his feet.

He realized he could use the dead whenever he wished, so long as he made certain that they couldn't talk about it afterward. Erik and the lead box had proven that.

Bonus Scene

Feeling better than he had in days, Stefan left the buried ghost behind, whistling on his way home.

Bonus Scene Chapter 7: A Painful Education

The house was dark when Stefan returned to it, and he paused at the back door. He listened, trying to hear his father's deep voice, or his mother's shrill one. Other than the normal noises, that of the refrigerator and those few ghosts who never seemed to stay silent, his parents seemed to be absent.

Stefan reflected on their schedule for the day but he didn't remember any auctions. There was always the chance that they had gone out to antique stores to see if they could find some new, unknown piece.

His stomach rumbled and Stefan opened the back door, slipping into the kitchen and easing the door shut behind him.

He went to the cabinet, took down a box of saltine crackers and ate a few. Stefan stacked a few more in his hand, put the food away and drifted out of the kitchen and into the hallway.

His mother stood by the front door.

A heartbeat later, the back door slammed closed and the heavy footsteps of his father stomped across the kitchen floor until Stefan knew the man stood behind him.

"Where's the sailor?" his mother demanded.

Stefan weighed his options and decided upon a half-truth.

"Gone," he said. "I tried to control him and he escaped."

His father shoved him, launching Stefan forward, the crackers scattering on the floor. He tried to get to his feet, to get to the stairs and escape his parents but he was too slow.

His mother moved forward with surprising speed, a small horsewhip in her hands. The thin piece of wood whistled in the air before it cracked against his back with a sharp, numbing pain.

Stefan rolled but his father stopped him and twisted him around so his chest was against the floor. He felt the man's large hands tear the shirt off his back, exposing Stefan's skin to his mother.

The horse whip struck him again and again, obtaining a sickly, despotic rhythm that wrenched screams from Stefan's throat.

"It is for your own good, Stefanushka," his father said with emotion, "these items are to be cared for and protected. Not abused or neglected. This punishment, my son, will help you remember what I say."

Through the pain, Stefan agreed.

He would never forget the lesson, or how to best repay his parents.

* * *

FREE Bonus Novel!

Wow, I hope you enjoyed this book as much as I did writing it! If you enjoyed the book, please leave a review. Your reviews inspire me to continue writing about the world of spooky and untold horrors!

To really show you my appreciation for downloading this book, please enjoy a **FREE extra spooky bonus novel.** This will surely leave you running scared!

Visit below to download your bonus novel and to learn about my upcoming releases, future discounts and giveaways: www.ScareStreet.com

FREE books (30 - 60 pages):
Ron Ripley (Ghost Stories)
1. Ghost Stories (Short Story Collection)
   www.scarestreet.com/ghost

A.I. Nasser (Supernatural Suspense)
2. Polly's Haven (Short Story)
   www.scarestreet.com/pollys
3. This is Gonna Hurt (Short Story)
   www.scarestreet.com/thisisgonna

Multi-Author Scare Street Collaboration
4. Horror Stories: A Short Story Collection
   www.scarestreet.com/horror

And experience the full-length novels (150 – 210 pages):
Ron Ripley (Ghost Stories)
1. Sherman's Library Trilogy (FREE via mailing list signup)
   www.scarestreet.com
2. The Boylan House Trilogy

www.scarestreet.com/boylantri
3. The Blood Contract Trilogy
www.scarestreet.com/bloodtri
4. The Enfield Horror Trilogy
www.scarestreet.com/enfieldtri

Moving In Series
5. **Moving In Series Box Set Books 1 - 3 (22% off)**
www.scarestreet.com/movinginbox123
6. Moving In (Book 1)
www.scarestreet.com/movingin
7. The Dunewalkers (Moving In Series Book 2)
www.scarestreet.com/dunewalkers
8. Middlebury Sanitarium (Book 3)
www.scarestreet.com/middlebury
9. **Moving In Series Box Set Books 4 - 6 (25% off)**
www.scarestreet.com/movinginbox456
10. The First Church (Book 4)
www.scarestreet.com/firstchurch
11. The Paupers' Crypt (Book 5)
www.scarestreet.com/paupers
12. The Academy (Book 6)
www.scarestreet.com/academy

Berkley Street Series
13. Berkley Street (Book 1)
www.scarestreet.com/berkley
14. The Lighthouse (Book 2)
www.scarestreet.com/lighthouse
15. The Town of Griswold (Book 3)
www.scarestreet.com/griswold
16. Sanford Hospital (Book 4)
www.scarestreet.com/sanford
17. Kurkow Prison (Book 5)
www.scarestreet.com/kurkow
18. Lake Nutaq (Book 6)
www.scarestreet.com/nutaq
19. Slater Mill (Book 7)
www.scarestreet.com/slater
20. Borgin Keep (Book 8)
www.scarestreet.com/borgin

21. Amherst Burial Ground (Book 9)
www.scarestreet.com/amherst

Hungry Ghosts Street Series
22. Hungry Ghosts (Book 1)
www.scarestreet.com/hungry

Haunted Collection Series
23. Collecting Death (Book 1)
www.scarestreet.com/collecting
24. Walter's Rifle (Book 2)
www.scarestreet.com/walter

Victor Dark (Supernatural Suspense)
25. Uninvited Guests Trilogy
www.scarestreet.com/uninvitedtri
26. Listen To Me Speak Trilogy
www.scarestreet.com/listentri

A.I. Nasser (Supernatural Suspense)
Slaughter Series
27. Children To The Slaughter (Book 1)
www.scarestreet.com/children
28. Shadow's Embrace (Book 2)
www.scarestreet.com/shadows
29. Copper's Keeper (Book 3)
www.scarestreet.com/coppers

The Sin Series
30. Kurtain Motel (Book 1)
www.scarestreet.com/kurtain
31. Refuge (Book 2)
www.scarestreet.com/refuge
32. Purgatory (Book 3)
www.scarestreet.com/purgatory

The Carnival Series
33. Blood Carousel(Book 1)
www.scarestreet.com/bloodcarousel

David Longhorn (Supernatural Suspense)
The Sentinels Series

34. Sentinels (Book 1)
www.scarestreet.com/sentinels
35. The Haunter (Book 2)
www.scarestreet.com/haunter
36. The Smog (Book 3)
www.scarestreet.com/smog

Dark Isle Series
37. Dark Isle (Book 1)
www.scarestreet.com/darkisle
38. White Tower (Book 2)
www.scarestreet.com/whitetower
39. The Red Chapel (Book 3)
www.scarestreet.com/redchapel

Ouroboros Series
40. The Sign of Ouroboros (Book 1)
www.scarestreet.com/ouroboros
41. Fortress of Ghosts (Book 2)
www.scarestreet.com/fortress
42. Day of The Serpent (Book 3)
www.scarestreet.com/serpent

Curse of Weyrmouth Series
43. Curse of Weyrmouth (Book 1)
www.scarestreet.com/weyrmouth
44. Blood of Angels (Book 2)
www.scarestreet.com/bloodofangels

Eric Whittle (Psychological Horror)
Catharsis Series
45. Catharsis (Book 1)
www.scarestreet.com/catharsis
46. Mania (Book 2)
www.scarestreet.com/mania
47. Coffer (Book 3)
www.scarestreet.com/coffer

Sara Clancy (Supernatural Suspense)
Dark Legacy Series

48. Black Bayou (Book 1)
   www.scarestreet.com/bayou
49. Haunted Waterways (Book 2)
   www.scarestreet.com/waterways
50. Demon's Tide (Book 3)
   www.scarestreet.com/demonstide
Banshee Series
51. Midnight Screams (Book 1)
   www.scarestreet.com/midnight
52. Whispering Graves (Book 2)
   www.scarestreet.com/whispering
53. Shattered Dreams (Book 3)
   www.scarestreet.com/shattered

Black Eyed Children Series
54. Black Eyed Children (Book 1)
   www.scarestreet.com/blackeyed
55. Devil's Rise (Book 2)
   www.scarestreet.com/rise
56. The Third Knock (Book 3)
   www.scarestreet.com/thirdknock

Keeping it spooky,
Team Scare Street

Made in the USA
San Bernardino, CA
08 August 2018

7012008